O9-BUA-714

"Cole, why me?" Maddy sighed. "I've got baggage. A lot of it. I'm prickly."

Cole chuckled and she felt the vibration of the sound through his chest and into her back. "You're not the only one with baggage," he admitted. Before she could ask what he meant, he continued on. "Listen, what happened to you just made you cautious. You're not prickly. You're scared. I would be, too."

They let the thought sit for a few minutes, and then Cole spoke again. "I don't know, Maddy. I got thinking about how you're young and pretty and so damned strong and then...and then I couldn't stop thinking about you."

She looked up into his face. "The last thing I was looking for was a date. Maybe it just snuck up on both of us."

She licked her lips, which suddenly felt dry, and saw his gaze drop to where her tongue had wet the surface. Desire surged through her, terrifying by its very presence and exhilarating at the same time.

"It snuck up on me for sure," he admitted quietly, smiling. "You snuck up on me."

Dear Reader,

I love Christmas. I really do. The lead-up of the last few weeks can be so stressful and busy but magical, too. We have a lot of traditions in our family, and now that my little ones aren't so little anymore, we've built up some good memories, too.

This book is a bit of a hat tip to those moments. The references to *Christmas Vacation* come from having watched it time after time until we can pretty much quote all the dialogue; the penguin who sings to the tune of "I'm a Little Teapot" actually exists. Singing carols during Christmas Eve service is one of my favorite memories from childhood right through to having my own kids attend. Even though they're nearly grown now, I still read *The Polar Express* and *'Twas The Night Before Christmas* aloud on Christmas Eve.

So here's to magical holiday moments with the people who mean the most to you. I hope this season brings you many opportunities to create new memories you can cherish forever.

Merry Christmas,

Donna

THE COWBOY'S CHRISTMAS FAMILY

—

DONNA ALWARD

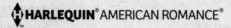

If you purchased this book without a cover you should be aware
that this book is stolen property. It was reported as "unsold and
destroyed" to the publisher, and neither the author nor the
publisher has received any payment for this "stripped book."

Recycling programs
for this product may
not exist in your area.

ISBN-13: 978-0-373-75591-2

The Cowboy's Christmas Family

Copyright © 2015 by Donna Alward

All rights reserved. Except for use in any review, the reproduction or
utilization of this work in whole or in part in any form by any electronic,
mechanical or other means, now known or hereinafter invented, including
xerography, photocopying and recording, or in any information storage
or retrieval system, is forbidden without the written permission of the
publisher, Harlequin Enterprises Limited, 225 Duncan Mill Road,
Don Mills, Ontario M3B 3K9, Canada.

This is a work of fiction. Names, characters, places and incidents are
either the product of the author's imagination or are used fictitiously,
and any resemblance to actual persons, living or dead, business
establishments, events or locales is entirely coincidental.

This edition published by arrangement with Harlequin Books S.A.

For questions and comments about the quality of this book,
please contact us at CustomerService@Harlequin.com.

® and TM are trademarks of Harlequin Enterprises Limited or its
corporate affiliates. Trademarks indicated with ® are registered in the
United States Patent and Trademark Office, the Canadian Intellectual
Property Office and in other countries.

Printed in U.S.A.

Donna Alward is a busy wife and mother of three (two daughters and the family dog), and she believes hers is the best job in the world: a combination of stay-at-home mom and romance novelist. An avid reader since childhood, Donna has always made up her own stories. She completed her arts degree in English literature in 1994, but it wasn't until 2001 that she penned her first full-length novel and found herself hooked on writing romance. In 2006, she sold her first manuscript, and now writes warm, emotional stories for Harlequin.

In her new home office in Nova Scotia, Donna loves being back on the east coast of Canada after nearly twelve years in Alberta, where her career began, writing about cowboys and the West. Donna's debut romance, *Hired by the Cowboy*, was awarded a Booksellers' Best Award in 2008 for Best Traditional Romance.

With the Atlantic Ocean only minutes from her doorstep, Donna has found a fresh take on life and promises even more great romances in the near future!

Donna loves to hear from readers. You can contact her through her website, donnaalward.com, or follow @DonnaAlward on Twitter.

Books by Donna Alward

Harlequin American Romance

Crooked Valley Ranch

The Cowboy's Christmas Gift
The Cowboy's Valentine
The Cowboy's Homecoming

Texas Rodeo Barons

The Texan's Baby

Cadence Creek Cowboys

Her Rancher Rescuer

Visit the Author Profile page
at Harlequin.com for more titles.

To my family—the reason for everything.

Chapter One

There were days when Madison Wallace felt like a single-mom Cinderella.

She blew at a few strands of hair that had escaped her messy ponytail, then tucked them behind her ears for at least the tenth time in the past half hour and checked her watch yet again.

Six twenty. The library closed at eight. The meeting was due to start in ten minutes and she didn't even have the coffeepot going yet. The boys were in a playpen in one of the smaller meeting rooms, and her brain was on the verge of shutdown, with her body not far behind.

Whoever came up with the idea of Snowflake Days needed their head examined.

Oh, right. That would be her.

Of course, she'd put forth that proposal last winter, and the mayor and council had loved the idea. She'd thought she'd have tons of time to help with the planning committee. The babies would be a little older, she'd be back at work, Gavin would be home at night to lend a hand, and life would be back to normal.

And then everything had changed.

She couldn't think about that now. She didn't have time. And playing the what-if game was a waste of energy, anyway.

The meeting room where the twins were was quiet except for the odd babble, so she rushed around as committee members started arriving and gathered in the foyer, chatting. There were twelve altogether, a blend of male and female, young and old, business owners and retirees and anything in between. She put tablets of paper at each spot at the conference table as well as pens that said Gibson Public Library on them. A separate table held coffee, now dripping merrily into the pot, ice water, and an array of muffins and breads, which she'd baked just this morning while the boys were napping rather than taking from the library's petty cash, which was always pretty tight.

"Maddy, this is just lovely, dear." Pauline Rowe stopped and patted her arm. "Thank you for setting it up. Now that Thanksgiving is over, we're really going to get into the nitty-gritty of the planning. Lots of coffee required."

Maddy smiled at Pauline, who owned the town's only dry cleaning and alterations shop. "Thanks, Pauline. Let me know if you need anything else, okay?"

An ear-splitting scream punctuated the relative quiet and Maddy winced. "Sorry. I'll be right back."

She rushed to the meeting room and found Liam and Lucas in the playpen. Liam was hanging on to the edge for dear life and crying, while Lucas whimpered softly in the corner, big crocodile tears on his cheeks.

Her boys. Best friends one moment, fighting like

cats the next, and at a year old, with no verbal skills to tell her what was wrong. She hadn't been prepared for motherhood, let alone times two. And going it alone? Since Gavin died, she'd really had to fight against despair at times. Like tonight, when she was bone weary.

"Hey, sweetie. Mama's here." She picked up Liam and settled him on her arm. He burrowed into her neck and stuck his thumb in his mouth, his wet face sticking to her skin. Her heart melted just a little bit. He was such a snuggle bug.

"You had to bring the twins?" Pauline asked gently. Without missing a beat, she went to the playpen and lifted out Lucas, who stared at her with owlish blue eyes and sucked in his lower lip as he fought against crying.

"Mom's down with the stomach flu as of this morning. It was…short notice to find a replacement."

Short notice was her excuse. The truth was, she didn't have the money to pay someone for child care today. It had come down to food and lights as far as priorities went. Filled tummies and running water were pretty important, and the holidays were coming.

She gave Liam a bounce and smiled, and he placed a chubby, if damp, hand on her cheek. Despite the troubles and challenges, she wouldn't trade her babies for anything. Things would work out the way they were supposed to. When times got rough, she found it difficult to remember that, but it was what she truly believed. Something good was around the corner for her. It was going to be okay. How could it not be?

"Hello, is the meeting in here?"

Maddy looked up and went dumb for a few seconds.

Cole Hudson, all six feet of him, stood in the doorway. He'd taken off his hat and held it in his hand…of course he had, because he had impeccable manners. His dark hair was cut short, just long enough for his fingers to leave trails as he ran his hand through it, in what Maddy assumed was a gesture of tidying it but really gave it a mussed look. And blue eyes. Blue with little crinkles at the corners. Like the Texas bluebells she'd seen once on a trip she'd taken with her parents.

A girl had to be blind not to get a little tongue-tied around Cole Hudson.

"Sorry," she said as she found her wits again. "The meeting's across the hall."

In her rush to get to the boys, the door to the meeting room had closed and locked, so she dug in her jeans pocket for the keys on one of those stretchy wrist things all the librarians used. She fumbled and Cole reached around, took the key from her hand and put it in the lock. He was standing awfully close to her, and she suddenly found it difficult to take a full breath.

"Allow me. You have your hands full," he said kindly, swinging open the door.

She adjusted Liam on her shoulder. "Let me get a door stopper so you don't get locked out again," she said, looking around, feeling unusually flustered. Pauline still held Lucas in her arms and he was starting to squirm, wanting to get down. Both boys were walking now, but unsteadily, which meant they were an accident waiting to happen when let loose.

She put the stopper in the door, committee members

started filing in—still chatting—and she took Lucas from Pauline, so she held a child in each arm.

"Is there anything more you need?" she asked the group at large, holding tight as Lucas twisted and fussed.

"We're fine, Maddy. Truly." Lacey Duggan came forward, a smile on her face. "This is wonderful. And you have your hands very full. We'll come find you if we need something, but really, don't worry about a thing."

"Thanks, Lacey." Lacey was new to Gibson, Montana, and new wife to Quinn Solomon up at Crooked Valley Ranch. Maddy let out a small sigh. "I was kind of hoping to be involved, but…" She let the sentence trail off and gave a small shrug with her aching shoulders.

"Your boys are adorable," Lacey added, ruffling Liam's hair.

"Thanks. I'm not usually this discombobulated." She boosted Lucas on her hip, getting him in a better position. "Work and babies don't go together very well."

"Everyone understands," Lacey offered sympathetically.

Yes, they did. And it burned Maddy's biscuits that she was reminded of it so very often. As if she could forget what had gotten her in this position in the first place.

Gavin had been a cheater. And a liar.

"Well, I'd better get back to the desk. Holler, okay?"

She pasted on a smile and went back to the room where she'd set up the boys. She dug in her bag and pulled out a sleeve of arrowroot cookies and two sippy cups of milk that had been sitting against an ice pack. "Okay, boys, please be good for Mommy. Please. I have to check the front desk and then I'll be back."

For the moment, the promise of a cookie and milk pacified the children and Maddy zipped out to the front desk. The library was quiet; other than the meeting there were no other special activities tonight, thank goodness. Two or three people browsed the stacks, and Maddy quietly went to them and told them to ring the bell at the circulation desk when they were ready to check their books out.

A quick breath and back to check on the boys.

And so went the next hour and a half. A quick check, back to the front. Change a diaper, back to the cart to put books back on the shelves. Slipping the twins into their pajamas, and then back to the drop box to scan the returned books into the system. She could hear the committee laughing behind the door and her shoulders slumped. She should be in there. She wanted to help. Last Christmas the boys had only been a month old. This year they were old enough to be excited at the bright lights and the sound of ripping paper, eating a real Christmas dinner even if half of it had to be mashed.

Maybe she could make next week's meeting. As long as her mom could babysit…

At five minutes to eight, the conference room door opened and the noise got louder, just as Liam had nodded off and Lucas was finally starting to settle, curled up with a blanket and rubbing his eyes. The sudden change in volume startled them both, and Maddy closed her eyes for a second, let out a breath. It was nearly done. She could close up the library and take the boys home and maybe, finally, get some sleep.

And for right now she was going to let the boys fuss and whimper for two minutes while she saw everyone out and locked the damn doors.

The place was nearly empty when she turned from the circulation desk and saw Cole come around the corner, a very grouchy Lucas on his arm. She felt a definite pang in her chest, seeing her fussy boy being held by a strong man, like a father would. Only Lucas didn't have a father. He was going to miss out on all of that.

Then there was the impact of seeing Cole Hudson holding a baby. Men and babies… Maddy didn't know if there was an evolutionary, biological reason for finding it so attractive or not, but there was no denying her heart softened just a little bit and her pulse started beating just a little faster.

"Cole, I'm sorry. I was going to get back to the boys as soon as I locked up." She gave a small smile. "It doesn't hurt them to fuss for a few minutes, you know."

"The other one's back to sleep. I thought I'd get this little guy out before he woke him up again." Cole smiled, and her heart went all mushy again.

Stop it, she reminded herself. *Pretty is as pretty does.* And Gavin had been darned pretty. He'd given her pretty babies. And in all likelihood he'd fathered another one that was due any day—Laura Jessup's baby.

She had a long way to go before she trusted anyone ever again. Even Cole, who had such a stellar reputation in the community that it seemed he could do no wrong.

"Thanks. I'll take him. You probably want to get going."

But Cole didn't move. "You're not leaving right away, are you?"

Her cheeks heated. "Well, I have to spend a few minutes tidying up. It won't take long."

Cole shifted Lucas's weight, and to Maddy's consternation, Lucas's eyes were drifting shut, cocooned in the warm curve of Cole's arm. "It'll take you longer if you have him in your arms," Cole reasoned. "I can stay for a few minutes. Give you a hand."

"That's generous of you, Cole, but…"

"But nothing." He chuckled. "I heard you were stubborn. Accept the help, Maddy. It's no big deal."

It felt like a big deal to her. "I'm perfectly capable of handling it. Thank you." She moved forward and took Lucas out of Cole's arms, close enough to Cole that she could smell his aftershave and feel the soft cotton of his shirt as her fingers brushed against it. The last thing she wanted was more pity. More sympathetic looks. All it did was remind her of how stupid she'd been. How duped. She'd been an inconsolable wreck when she'd gotten the news about the car accident. Three days later she'd gone to Gavin's funeral as the grieving widow, devastated that they'd never have the chance to fix their marriage, that her boys would grow up without their father.

And two days later she'd heard the rumors. And remembered that Laura had been at the funeral and offered her condolences…

Maddy brushed past Cole and left him to exit the library on his own, and she went to the conference room and began putting muffins back in the tin with one hand.

No one would make a fool of her that way again.

COLE SAT AT the kitchen table, sipping a glass of water and reading one of his latest cattle magazines. He knew he should go to bed. Tomorrow was an early start, and there were things he wanted to get done before snow hit, as it was forecast to do tomorrow night. He turned another page and realized he hadn't really been reading. He'd been thinking about Maddy Wallace, how tired she'd looked, how she tried to cover it with her work face and how defensive she'd gotten when he'd tried to help.

And then he'd called her stubborn and that had been the end of any assistance he might have offered. That really stuck in her craw. He'd make a point of not saying that again. He was certain to see her, as the meetings for the committee were always at the library. Besides, Gibson was pretty small. Their paths crossed now and again.

And as such, Maddy's story was pretty common knowledge. Her husband had been killed in a car accident several months before, leaving her widowed with the twins. Which would have been bad enough, but rumors had spread that Gavin Wallace had been having an affair. He didn't blame Maddy for being defensive. It wasn't nice having your dirty laundry hung up for everyone to see.

The exhausted, hopeless look on her face tonight had reminded him of someone else, too. Someone he tried not to think of much anymore…

He hardly noticed when his mother came into the kitchen. It wasn't until the fridge door opened that he jumped and spun in his chair, looking over his shoulder at her.

Ellen Hudson was still a beautiful woman at fifty-seven. Her gray hair was cut in a wispy sort of bob and while she had crow's-feet at the corners of her eyes, they still twinkled as blue as ever. She gave a light laugh at Cole's surprise and took a carton of milk from the fridge.

"You're up late. I didn't mean to scare you."

"Just reading. Winding down." Thinking too much.

She went to the cupboard and got a mug. "Me, too. I couldn't sleep so I thought I'd try some warm milk." She poured the milk into the mug and put it in the microwave. Cole watched as she took it out again, added a splash of vanilla and a spoon of brown sugar, and took a sip.

"I don't know how you drink that disgusting stuff," he commented, closing his magazine.

She grinned and sat down opposite him. "I drank it when I was pregnant with Tanner and was off the caffeine." She cradled the mug and looked up at him. "Something on your mind, son?"

"Not really. Probably just too much coffee at the meeting tonight."

"How'd that go?"

"Good," he answered, leaning back in his chair. "Things are coming together."

"I'm sorry we're going to miss it," his mother said. "We'll be in St. Thomas by then."

Cole grinned. "You're not that sorry. You and Dad have been waiting for this trip for years." They were flying to Florida to spend a week, and then taking a two-week cruise through the Caribbean. "Besides, you'll be back for Christmas."

"Of course we will. With a suntan." She laughed a little. "I'm not sure if my sleeping problems are from excitement or anxiety."

It was Cole's turn to laugh. "Mom, I promise Tanner and I aren't going to throw any ragers while you guys are out of town."

"Smart-ass." But she laughed, too. "You both are grown men. And good men. Still, I hate leaving you to manage both the ranch and the house."

"We're big boys. We know how to clean and cook. You go and don't worry a bit about us. We'll eat steak every night. It's Tanner's specialty."

If Tanner was ever home, that was. He always seemed to find somewhere to go, something to do. And when he wasn't being a social butterfly, he was putting in hours as a volunteer EMT. Maybe it was because Tanner was younger, but he had an energy that far surpassed Cole's. Or maybe Cole was just more of a homebody.

"You know, if you'd hurry up and get married…"

"I know, I know. You and Dad would downsize and you wouldn't worry about me so much. And while I'm at it, get to work on some grandkids for you to spoil."

It was a well-worn refrain. And one he understood, but he didn't need to have it mentioned quite so often. It wasn't that he had anything against settling down. He just hadn't met the right one yet. Every girl he dated seemed great for a while, but then the novelty fizzled out.

Lately he'd started to wonder if the problem was that he was afraid of getting too close to someone. When Roni left him, he'd felt like such a failure. He'd tried over and over to help her, but nothing had worked. He had no idea where she was now, or if she was even okay. Truth be told, he hadn't been in love with a woman since she'd trampled on his heart. And that had been eight long years ago.

His mind went back a few hours to Maddy and the way she'd shut him out so quickly. She was living proof of what happened when a marriage went wrong. The last thing he'd want to do was rush into a marriage and end up making a mess. "I'm not in a big hurry," he replied, frowning into his water glass. "I take marriage seriously, Mom. Isn't that what you want?"

"Of course." She reached over and touched his hand. "You know we just want to see you happy. You'd be such a good dad, Cole. A good husband. You're a good man."

Ugh, she made it sound as though he was such a paragon, when he knew he wasn't. He supposed she was looking at him through mom goggles.

"Hmm," he answered, thinking again of Maddy and how stressed she'd seemed. It had to be hard at the best of times, handling twins. Doing it on her own must be an extra challenge. He remembered what she was like before. A hard worker, always with a smile, with an extra glow once she met Gavin and they got engaged. In Gibson everyone pretty well knew everyone else, even though she'd been a few years behind him in school. It sucked that her vibrancy, that glow, had disappeared.

"Thinking about anything in particular?" his mom asked.

"Just Maddy Wallace. She was working at the library tonight and her babysitting fell through and she had the twins. She was run ragged."

"Maddy's had a rough time, that's for sure." She nodded. "Losing her husband, finding out he was cheating. She's one strong girl, picking herself up the way she has. But the whole situation has to be hard."

"I got the impression that she doesn't appreciate a lot of pity," he said, raising an eyebrow.

"Would you?" his mom asked simply. "If your dad had stepped out on me, and the whole town knew about it? I'd be humiliated. And really angry. Honey, Maddy hasn't got anyone to be angry with anymore, except herself, really. I'm sure she'd rather forget all about the whole thing."

He hadn't thought of it in quite that way before. The one person she'd probably like to ask most about the affair couldn't answer. And as far as he could gather, Laura wasn't talking. Which was to her credit, really. But it didn't help stop the gossip.

"Son," she said, taking the last drink of her milk, "this is one time I'm not going to do any urging or matchmaking. Maddy has a truckload of baggage to sort through. But if you ended up in a position to give her a helping hand, that wouldn't be amiss, either. The holidays are coming up and she has those two babies to think about. Maybe your committee can think about that, too, amid all the festival stuff."

It wasn't a half-bad idea, though the idea of Maddy accepting any form of charity was ludicrous. She wouldn't even accept his help in cleaning up the room tonight, which was just dumping some garbage cans and emptying the coffeemaker.

It would have to be something secret, something she wouldn't expect, something that seemed random.

What in heck would that be?

"I'm a guy. I don't do well with this sort of thing."

His mom laughed, got up and put her mug in the sink. Then she came over to him and dropped a kiss on top of his head. "You're probably better at it than you think. And now I have to get to bed. I have a lot of packing to do tomorrow. I'm not letting your father anywhere near those suitcases."

After she left the room, Cole fussed with the corner of the magazine pages, thinking. It wasn't a bad idea, actually, helping one of their own. Besides, up until the last few months, Maddy had always been active in Gibson, helping out with fund-raisers and activities with a smile.

Life had handed her some huge lemons. Maybe it was up to them to give her the lemonade. It was the season of giving, after all.

What could go wrong?

Chapter Two

Maddy was trying to space out her shopping and minimize her babysitting bills, so she hit the town's rather small department store on a Tuesday after work to pick up a few things before she was due to get the boys.

She had forty dollars today. That was it. And there was another payday before Christmas where she might be able to squeeze a bit more out of her check. It wasn't as though the boys were old enough to know they were getting less than most other kids. It was that *she* knew. She knew she couldn't provide the type of Christmas she wanted to and it bugged her to no end.

As she pushed the metal cart toward the baby section, she took a deep breath. Thinking about finances just made her angry at Gavin again, and that didn't serve any purpose. In the new year, she was going to make a new plan, that was all. Maybe downsize to a smaller house, for one. The three of them didn't need two thousand square feet, really. A smaller bungalow would suit them fine and the upkeep would certainly be easier.

She stopped by the baby clothes, searching for discounts. Pajamas were on sale, cute little blue and green ones with the feet in them and a brown-and-white puppy on the front. She put one of each color in the cart. She picked up fuzzy socks, new slippers with the traction dots on the bottom and two soft white onesies.

Calculating in her head, she had about fifteen dollars left. Barely.

At the toy section she was utterly daunted. How could she buy two toys with what she had left?

She'd decided on the rock-a-stack rings she knew the boys loved from the church nursery, and was deliberating the wisdom of wooden alphabet blocks when a voice startled her.

"I just need help getting it down from the top shelf."

Maddy looked across the aisle and felt her face go red-hot. Laura Jessup was smiling at an employee, pointing at a crib set on a high shelf. She was everything Maddy wasn't, it seemed—petite, red haired, creamy complexioned, young.

And carrying Maddy's husband's baby. There was no mistaking the roundness at her middle. At Maddy's best guess, Laura had to be close to seven, eight months along. Not that she was about to ask the exact due date. Gavin had died five months ago, which meant that he'd been seeing Laura pretty much since she'd showed up in town last spring.

With the plastic case containing the comforter in hand, Laura turned around and caught Maddy staring at her. For a brief second she looked embarrassed and awkward, but then she put on an uncertain smile. "Madison," she began, and started walking toward Maddy.

Hell, no, Maddy thought, her throat tightening and heart pounding. *This is not going to happen.*

She wasn't going to have a panic attack, but it was damned close, and she hustled the cart across to housewares, down the center and straight to the cash registers.

A quick glance behind her as she put her items on the belt reassured her that Laura hadn't followed her. Thank God. Maddy wasn't interested in anything Laura had to say.

"Is that all today, Mrs. Wallace?"

She nodded at the girl behind the counter. Young and fresh faced and wearing a Santa hat, she looked innocent and happy. "Yes, that's it, Stephanie. Thanks."

"It's forty-one dollars and ten cents," Stephanie said, and Maddy dug out the extra dollar and change. She'd stayed pretty close to budget after all.

"Is the library still having the tree lighting?" the cashier asked, chatting as if unaware that Maddy wanted to be just about anywhere else right now.

"Yes, on the thirteenth," she answered. "To kick off Snowflake Days."

"It's so much fun every year. Last year when I went, I—"

Maddy grabbed the shopping bags and flashed a hurried smile. "Sorry, Stephanie. I was supposed to pick up the boys ten minutes ago. I've gotta run."

"Oh, sure, Mrs. Wallace. Have a nice day."

The air outside the store was bitter, a distinct change from the crisp bite of earlier. It felt as if snow was in the air. She'd like to get home before it started, since she didn't have her winter tires on yet. She should probably do that soon...

"Afternoon, Maddy."

She had her head stuck in the trunk, stowing the bags, and the sound of her name being spoken prompted her to stand up too quickly and smack her head on the hood.

She now understood why people called it seeing stars. Little dots swam in front of her eyes as she held on to the lip of the trunk for support.

"Whoa, there!" A strong hand gripped her arm, steadying her. "I didn't mean to scare you. Sorry about that."

She blinked a few times and her vision cleared, though the pain was still sharp in her head. Cole Hudson stood before her, a frown of concern on his handsome face.

"I'm fine. You just scared me, is all." She pushed away from the car, and then reached for the hood, giving it a good slam.

"Maddy, hold still." He reached into his pocket and took out a handkerchief. "I think you cut your head."

Now that he mentioned it, there was a funny feeling on the right side of her head, as if a raindrop had fallen on her hair and was trickling toward her ear.

He reached forward and pressed the cotton to her head with a firm but gentle touch. "Wow, you really smacked it."

He took the handkerchief away and she saw a decent-sized blot of blood. "I've been preoccupied all day," she admitted, letting out a breath. "And I'm late to pick up the boys." It was a white lie, but he didn't know that.

It sounded better than *I'm running away from my husband's mistress.*

"I want to make sure you're all right first," Cole insisted. "Or I could drive you over there myself. They at your folks' place?"

"No, at the day care. I can't expect Mom to keep them all the time, and it was a workday for me. Besides, the day care is closer." Maddy's mom and dad lived on a pretty lot on the other side of the river. They'd been absolutely wonderful over the past few months, but Maddy was determined to stand on her own two feet.

He dabbed at her head with the kerchief again. "It seems to be stopping. Not too deep, then. Still, it looks like you had your bell rung pretty good."

He'd raised one eyebrow and looked slightly roguish, a small smile flirting with his lips. She couldn't help it—she laughed a little. "So, my secret is out. Now you know I'm the world's biggest klutz."

"Oh, I wouldn't say that big." He was genuinely smiling at her now. "Listen, I've been meaning to call you. I wanted to talk to you about the festival. Why don't we grab a coffee or something?"

It surprised her to realize that she wanted to accept. Generally she took her own tea bags or hot chocolate to the library rather than spend money on the extravagance, and she really did need to pick up the boys… though it had been a complete fabrication to say she was running late, since she was paid up until five, which was another hour and a bit away.

"I probably shouldn't," she said, pushing her purse straps more securely on her shoulder.

"Hey," Cole said quietly. "When was the last time you let someone buy you a cup of coffee, huh? It's got to be hard being a single mom. Heck, my ma raised two boys and she had my dad and she said we were exhausting. You've got twins…phew."

"Great, now I'm a pity date?"

"Good Lord, woman, you're exasperating." Cole stepped back and tucked his hands into his jacket pockets. "I actually do want to talk to you about the festival. Over coffee sounded kind of nice, that's all. Look, I admire all your independence and stuff, but not everything comes from pity around here. Sometimes people genuinely want to help people they care about, that's all."

Was he saying he cared about her? They didn't even know each other that well. Of course, he must be speaking in far more general terms, right?

His words made her feel sheepish, too. It was no secret she had a chip on her shoulder. She'd always liked Cole. He was well-known in town, and had been only a couple of years ahead of her in school. He and Gavin had been in the same class from kindergarten right through graduation. Not that she truly trusted Gav's judgment anymore, either.

She sighed, met Cole's gaze. "I get defensive. I'm sorry, Cole. I was kind of stressed out when you came up behind me and then I whacked my head and you're right about the pity thing." She shrugged. "I tell myself every day that I should get over being bitter. It's just hard."

"Of course it is. And you're bringing up two rambunctious boys on your own. You'll find people in this town have a lot of respect for you, Maddy. Now what do you say? Do you want to stop at the diner, or maybe the Daily Grind?"

Why shouldn't she go have a cup of something? Didn't she deserve something for herself? Maddy nodded and felt a weight lift. "The Grind would be really nice, actually. I haven't been in there for ages."

She locked the car and walked beside him as they made their way down Main Street to the coffee shop. It had opened fairly recently, a somewhat trendy spot in a town steeped in old-time traditions. He held the door for her and she stepped in, loving the scents that hit her nose the moment she entered—coffee, chocolate, cinnamon—lovely, cozy, warm scents that wrapped around her and eased some of the stresses of her day.

"What will you have?" Cole asked. "My treat."

"I can get my own," she insisted, but Cole cut her off.

"What did I just say outside?"

"Sorry." She hoped she wasn't blushing again. "Um, what kinds of tea do you have?" She looked at the girl behind the counter.

"The list is here." The girl gestured, pointing to a sign on a glass display front. "But this month we have a special flavor called Country Christmas, if you would like to try it. It's kind of like mulled cider, only with black tea."

"That sounds lovely. I'll have that," Maddy said. She looked longingly at the apple cinnamon pastries, but it would only be a few more hours and she'd have dinner. Besides, she was letting Cole buy her tea. She wouldn't presume to order anything to eat.

He ordered coffee and Maddy added honey to her tea while he waited for his order. To her surprise, he came over to her and put down a plate with two pastries on it before reaching for the cream to add to his coffee.

"Don't say it," he said before she could even open her mouth. "My mom and dad left a few days ago for their trip and there's no baking in the house."

"Let me guess. Chronic sweet tooth?"

He stirred his coffee, dropped the stir stick in the trash and picked up both mug and plate. "Yeah. I think I'm spoiled probably, because my mom always keeps the kitchen well stocked for us."

"Hungry boys working the ranch need good home cooking."

"Yep." He grinned. "And my mom's is the best."

They found seats not too far from the window. Maddy looked around. The Christmas decorations were up, with boughs and pretty white lights draped around the dark wood rails and beams. Someone had sprayed fake snow on the corners of the windows, and a huge poinsettia was on a small table in the corner. Some sort of new-agey Christmas music played on the speakers, with a bluesy-sounding saxophone and a reassuring bass line. Maddy took a sip of her tea—delicious—and let her stress levels drop another notch.

"See?" he said, pushing the plate toward her and handing her one of the forks. "Time out for Maddy."

She laughed a bit. "I've been so cranky lately that you're probably doing a public service," she joked. Sort of joked, anyway. All work and no play and all that...

"Aw, darn, you saw right through me," he quipped, cutting a huge corner of the pastry with the edge of his fork. "Of course not. I just realized last week at the library that you really had your hands full. It got me thinking, that's all."

Again she got the weird swirly sensation at the idea of Cole thinking about *her*.

"Well, whatever the reason, thank you. This is delicious."

"That's better. And you're welcome."

She took a bite of turnover and closed her eyes. The pastry was light and flaky and beautifully buttery. "This is going to ruin my supper, and I don't even care," she said, licking the caramelly residue on the fork.

"I'd say mine, too, but it's Tanner's night to cook. If he's home. I'll probably end up making myself a sandwich or something later tonight."

"Your mom really does spoil you." She met his gaze again and grinned.

"And I let her, so I'm as bad as she is." He smiled, too. "Honestly, there are some pros to still living at home. And it doesn't make sense to pay for two households when there's more than enough room. But yeah, I'm a thirty-three-year-old man living with his parents. Whooee, look at me."

Maddy wondered why he'd never married, but she sure as shootin' wasn't going to ask. It was none of her business, and she didn't like it when people pried into her personal life. Besides, Cole was hardly the stereotypical live-at-home type. The Hudson ranch was solid, respected in the town and state, with a reputation for quality stock and fair dealing. Definitely a family operation.

Before she could reply, he continued, "Of course,

there are some disadvantages, too. Like no privacy. And it can be a little tough on the ego."

"You've got big shoulders," she said, cutting off another bite of pastry. "You can handle it. If I remember right from our school days, you always seemed to handle just about anything."

He'd had a reputation then of being solid, stable, smart. Reliable. The girls all swooned over him, he was well liked in general and he'd never gotten into any trouble, to her recollection. His brother, on the other hand…

"Wow. Maybe I should check my back to see if I've sprouted wings."

"Naw, you could just take out another hanky and polish your halo."

He laughed again. "How is your head, anyway?"

She touched the spot gingerly. "Tender, but not bad. Just a teensy goose egg."

"Good."

They each drank again and then Maddy put down her cup and pushed the plate aside. "So, you said you wanted to ask me something about the festival. What can I do to help? I know I haven't been much help on the committee."

Cole nodded. "Well, we're looking for volunteers. I don't know what your plans are with regard to the boys, but I thought I'd mention a few things. If it's too hard on your schedule, maybe you could suggest someone."

"Okay."

"First up is the night of the tree lighting. We're planning a food drive and need someone to just keep things organized at the collection site. When it's over, I've offered my truck to load up the food, and I'll deliver it the following day."

Maddy thought for a minute. "I'm going to take the twins, but I know my parents always go to it, too. I'll double-check with them to make sure they can watch the boys."

"That's great. The volunteers are all parking in the side lot at the fire station to free up room for attendees."

Maddy really wished she'd been able to sit in on the meetings. "That's a good idea. It's so close but will help with congestion."

"It was Mike Palmer's idea." Mike was part of the fire department and sat on just about every committee in Gibson. Maddy wasn't surprised.

"Your name came up when we were discussing another event, too." He finished his coffee and put the empty mug down on the table. "The Duggans have offered a wagon and horse team to do a sleigh ride on the walking pathway."

"A sleigh ride with wheels?" She smiled a little, and despite her earlier Scrooginess, she was intrigued.

"If we get a big dump of snow, Duke says they can drive the team down Main Street instead. So far there's only about an inch on the path. The idea is to leave from the library, go past the bridge down to the park, turn around and come back, and then have hot cocoa and cookies and story time inside. You're good with kids. Are you up for a sleigh ride and storytelling?"

It sounded magical. Maybe too magical. Still, the idea of bundling up the boys and taking them on a wagon ride with jingling bells and carols...maybe she couldn't have piles of presents under the tree, but they could still enjoy the season.

"Someone would have to stay at the library to make the cocoa and set out the cookies."

"Pauline's offered to do that. She has it all planned out. Sleigh ride at two, cocoa at two forty-five, story at three."

Maddy smiled again. "She is always so organized. She's a good chair for this event."

"I hear you're the one who did up the proposal last year," Cole said, his voice a bit softer. "You planned to be on the committee, didn't you?"

"Yeah." She looked up at him. "Hey, if I've learned anything this year, it's that sometimes things don't work out exactly as you planned."

"I'm really sorry about that, Maddy."

"Me, too. It is what it is."

Cole hesitated, but she could tell he wanted to say something. "What is it?" she asked. "You might as well say it. You won't hurt my feelings. I'm past that."

His gorgeous blue eyes held hers. "I was just wondering how you're managing, that's all. It's none of my business, I know that." He raised his hand as if to say, *tell me to back off if I'm overstepping.* "It's just… I don't know what I'm trying to say. Well, I do, but I know how you feel about pity and charity."

Embarrassment slithered through her stomach, crept up her chest and neck in the form of a blush. "We're getting by, so don't worry about that. In the new year I'm going to sit down and make some decisions, I think. But we're not cold and we're not starving, Cole. There are others out there a lot worse off than we are." Who was she to complain? Her children had clothes and food and love and a roof over their heads. More than anything, Maddy had learned that the rest was just gravy. Window dressing. She knew she needed to spend a lot more time being thankful and less time being bitter.

"Maybe you could use some extra cash for Christmas?"

"What do you mean?" She frowned. "I considered looking for some extra retail shifts in town for a few weeks, just during the busy time. But by the time I factored in child care…it didn't seem worth it."

"What if you could take the boys with you and didn't have to pay for day care?"

She laughed. "What employer would go along with that?"

He leveled his gaze at her. "I would."

"You?"

The idea of working for Cole Hudson was so strange and, frankly, made her stomach flip over nervously. "Cole, if this is some make-work project to, I don't know, make you feel good or something…"

Something flitted through his eyes, but then she wondered if she'd imagined it, it was gone so fast. "It's not," he assured her. "Tanner and I are on our own until the twenty-third. I'm a terrible cook and Tanner's unreliable, frankly. I can't eat fried steak every night for three weeks. I was thinking that I'd like to hire someone just until then, to come in and do some cooking and light cleaning every other day or so. Without Dad, Tanner and I are putting in some extra hours. Not having to do the wash or make dinner at night would be awesome."

"You want a housekeeper."

"I just thought, since you're part-time at the library, and with Christmas coming up, it might work out well for you. I'll pay ten bucks an hour, for four hours every other day."

The annoying thing was that he was right and the temptation of the money was great. Still, it was a pity job, wasn't it? And that grated.

She wasn't sure she had room for pride right now. Forty dollars a day times, what, eight days? That was three hundred and twenty dollars. She could buy the boys' presents for sure, and have leftover to catch up on bills. How could she say no to that?

He tapped her hand, bringing her attention back. "Hey," he said. "I can probably hire a student who's home for Christmas to do it. But I thought of you. And you can bring the boys with you. I don't mind."

"You'd want me to tidy up, do laundry, do some cooking?"

"That's it. It would be helping us out a lot, and maybe giving you some fun money at the same time. Win-win."

"I never saw myself as a housekeeper," she muttered. "Not that there's anything wrong with that. I'm not too proud for it. I just…well, damn, Cole. My life has just done a one eighty in the last few months. It's like I hardly recognize it anymore."

Cole put his hand over hers. "It's okay. When something so unexpected happens, so life altering, it takes a good while to adjust to a new normal."

The knot of tension eased inside her. His hand felt warm and strong over hers, and his words were exactly what she needed to hear. Rather than looking at her life as a chaotic mess, it was a search for a new normal. She'd get there. She just had to be patient.

"When would you want me to start?"

He laughed. "Tomorrow? Three days and I'm already sick of Tanner's cooking and the laundry's piling up."

She checked her watch, realizing that time had flown and she truly did have to pick up the boys soon. "Would mornings be okay? I usually work afternoons at the library, and on my days off I'd still be able to get the boys home for a good afternoon nap. You have no idea how much that helps their temperament."

"Mornings are fine. I'll leave the front door open, but I'll try to be in around…nine? I'll show you around, get you set up. Then you're done by one."

"Sounds good." She pushed out her chair and reached for her coat. "I really should get going, though. The day care gets miffed if parents are late. But thank you for the tea. You were right. It was nice to just get out and sit for an hour or so."

"It was my pleasure. And thanks for helping me out." He stood and took his jacket off the back of his chair. In moments they were bundled up against the cold and headed for the door.

To her surprise, he walked her back to her car, too. The snow had started, just light flakes drifting lazily, and Maddy hoped they didn't get much. She had to drive out to Cole's in the morning, and without winter tires.

Maybe the first thing she should do with Cole's money was have them installed.

He shut her door for her and waited until she'd started the car before stepping back. Maybe she should feel crowded or patronized by his behavior this afternoon. But she didn't.

She felt cared for and protected. Which was silly. It was a few hours of work, and a request for volunteering, and a cup of tea. And she was fully capable of looking after herself.

But it was the fact that he'd looked at her—really at her—that had made the difference. And she didn't think he'd simply seen Maddy Wallace, charity case.

If nothing else, she was extremely grateful for that.

Chapter Three

Cole knew he shouldn't be nervous.

So why was his gut a tangle of knots? He'd come to the house at eight thirty, after the first of the morning chores were done, and he'd washed up, combed his hair—twice—and considered changing his shirt.

It was just Maddy. He'd known her his whole life. And this was just his way of helping her out over the holidays. It was funny, he realized, that the whole committee for Snowflake Days talked about helping the less fortunate at Christmas but Maddy's name hadn't come up once. It didn't take a genius to do the math. Unless Gavin had left her a hefty life-insurance policy—which Cole doubted he had—part-time hours at a small municipal library wouldn't house and feed a family of three. Plus day care. Maddy had to be struggling, and far more than she let on.

She wouldn't accept help, so offering her work was really the only solution. He didn't even really need it. He knew how to run a washing machine and a vacuum perfectly well. And he wasn't the greatest cook, but he could bake a potato, make a chicken breast, heat some vegetables in the microwave. Hell, last night he'd gone into the market and picked up one of those rotisserie chicken meals for fifteen dollars and it had done him and Tanner for supper and there were still leftovers in the fridge.

He wasn't as inept as he'd led her to believe, but she didn't need to know that.

Movement out the front window caught his attention and he looked closer, saw her car crawling carefully up the drive. Fool woman still had her summer tires on, and it was December. With the three inches of snow that had fallen last night, the road probably had tricky spots.

Cole ran his hand over his hair once more before reaching for the doorknob. He swung it open just as she climbed the steps, carrying a diaper bag and playpen in her arms.

"Thanks!" she huffed out, putting them down just inside the kitchen. "Just a sec. I'll get the boys."

Her head disappeared inside the car again, and when she withdrew she had a boy on each arm. At least it looked like the boys—the snowsuits in blue and red were so puffy that Cole could hardly see the babies inside.

It occurred to him that she must have really great biceps, and he grinned at the thought.

"Here, let me take one of them," he offered as she climbed the steps. She leaned to one side, handing him one of the boys—he couldn't tell which one. Once inside she sat her cargo on the floor and began the process of pulling off boots and unzipping snowsuits. Cole hadn't done such a thing ever in his life, but he followed her lead, and before too long two identical boys stood before them dressed in little jogging suits with crooked socks and staticky hair, a pile of winter gear at their feet.

"How do you tell them apart?" Cole asked. "I mean, as their mom, you must just know or something. But… well, how do I tell the difference?"

She laughed. "Luke is a little bigger than Liam, and his eyes are just a little different. He's more independent, too. Liam's the one who likes to cuddle and be held all the time." She looked over at him and her eyes twinkled. "Which means one is in my arms, making it hard for me to get anything done, and the other one is off getting into trouble—"

"Making it hard for you to get anything done." Cole chuckled. "I get it." He looked directly at the boys and nodded. "Hi, Luke. Hi, Liam."

They both stared at him with owl eyes, but one raised a hand and opened and shut his fingers in a sort of wave. The other popped his thumb in his mouth.

"So this one is Luke," he said, pointing at the waver, "and the other is Liam."

"Bingo. Let me set up the playpen and get them into a confined space, and then you can show me where things are."

It seemed to take no time at all and she had the playpen set up. A few solid jerks and snaps and it popped into a square. Without any fuss she deposited the boys inside, added a handful of soft toys from the bag she'd brought, gathered up their outerwear and stowed it neatly on a bench by the door, and was ready to go.

"Are you sure they'll be okay there?" Cole was skeptical. It seemed like such a small space, after all.

But Maddy nodded. "I'm sure. Until they're not, and I'll deal with that when we get there." She smiled at him. "Okay. Give me the nickel tour."

He led her through the house, showing her the upstairs first, where the bedrooms and bathrooms were. "The washer and dryer are in the mudroom off the garage," he said. "Tanner and I put our dirty laundry there this morning, but normally we keep it in a clothes hamper in our rooms."

On the way downstairs he added, "Mom keeps her cleaning supplies in the laundry room, too, in a carry basket. You should be able to find everything you need there."

"Sounds fine," she said, following behind him.

They went to the mudroom next and he opened a closet to reveal a vacuum cleaner and broom and dustpan. "For the floors. The big freezer is out here, too, if you start supper or anything and are looking for stuff."

They ventured back into the kitchen. To Cole's surprise, the boys were stacking up soft blocks on the floor of the playpen and then knocking them over, giggling. It took no time at all to give her the rundown of the cupboards. "I'd better go and get out of your way, then," he added, feeling suddenly awkward. He couldn't help but notice she'd worn a soft hoodie in dark green, a color that set off her fair skin and blue eyes. And Maddy Wallace looked damned fine in a pair of dark-wash jeans, too. He had the sudden thought that she'd be very nice to cuddle up to…

"Hey, are you okay?" Her voice interrupted him. "You just kind of drifted off there for a sec."

Could he feel more foolish? He remembered his mom's words a few days before they left, when he'd mentioned Maddy's name. She'd actually discouraged him from any romantic notions where Maddy was concerned. And after speaking to Maddy yesterday, he knew for sure that she was still hurting from the events of the last year. He had no business thinking about being near her in any way other than being a good neighbor.

"I'm fine. Sorry."

"It's no problem. Will you and Tanner be in for lunch?"

She was all business, and he should be glad, but he was a little annoyed. Clearly she wasn't as distracted by him as he was by her.

"Yes, around noon or a little after. But we can get ourselves something to eat."

"Let's just see how it goes." She smiled at him. "I'll be fine, Cole. I'm going to start some laundry before the boys start demanding attention, and I think I'll run the vacuum over the floors and get some cooking started."

"Right." It was what he'd hired her to do, but he had to admit it felt strange, having her and her babies in the middle of the normally quiet house. And not strange in a bad way, necessarily. Just very, very different.

While she traded toys for the boys in the playpen, Cole went to the mudroom and put on his jacket and boots. He had his hand on the doorknob when she appeared, heading straight for the two laundry hampers standing in front of the dryer.

She laughed. "Seriously, Cole. I can run a washing machine."

He shook his head. "Sorry. I don't know what's wrong with me today. Of course you can. I'll see you in a few hours. I'll be at the barn if you need anything."

"If you keep talking, you'll be here until lunch. And I won't get any work done."

He swallowed against the lump in his throat, annoyed with the route his thoughts had taken. That wasn't what this was about. It was helping someone who needed a hand. Nothing more.

He stomped outside and shut the door behind him, then hurried through the snow to the barn. Maybe the fresh air would get his head right. In any case, he'd better get himself together for when he went back to the house at noon.

MADDY BREATHED A sigh of relief as Cole left the house. She could see him walking to the barn, his hands shoved in his jacket pockets and his shoulders hunched against the cold. He'd lingered this morning, and she wasn't sure what for, but there'd been a moment in the kitchen when his eyes had gone all soft and dazed and little alarm bells had gone off in her head.

Cole was a nice guy. He was giving her a helping hand and she appreciated it. But oh, my, she was so not in a place for romance. She hoped that wasn't what he had on his mind. She had her hands full enough just trying to keep her life together.

It didn't help that he was so flipping handsome, either. Stupid dark hair that set off his stupid blue eyes so that a girl couldn't think straight. Well, she was smarter than that now, and her only reason for being here was to make a little extra Christmas cash to give her sons a special holiday.

Speaking of, she needed to get that load of laundry in the washer if she was going to get two loads done in the time she had left.

By the time she'd sorted the clothes and gotten the washer started, the boys were getting bored. She took them out of the playpen, and then moved the bulky structure to the stairs, blocking them from doing any climbing—and falling. Then she turned on the television and found the station and programs that they liked. Even at barely over a year old, the sounds and colors were intriguing and Maddy laughed to herself as Liam bobbed on his knees a bit, out of time to the music but dancing, anyway. Luke took one look at his brother and joined in with a big toothy smile.

"Please, stay this good," she breathed as she spread out a blanket and added toys, making it a play mat in the middle of the living room.

In deference to Cole's professed sweet tooth, she wanted to bake something for them to have on hand, and she figured a cake was as fast as anything. It didn't take long to find a recipe book and the ingredients in Ellen's tidy cupboards, and while the boys played and sang away to the program on TV, she whipped up a chocolate cake and had it in the oven. A quick trip to the mudroom showed the laundry on the spin cycle, so she searched the freezer and took out a ham and put it in a slow cooker to bake for the afternoon. By the time she'd changed laundry over, the boys needed diaper changes and then a snack. The cake came out of the oven and she put it to cool, then sat with the boys for a few minutes and read them three stories, including their favorite, *Mole in a Hole*, twice.

After settling them again with a Thomas the Tank Engine DVD, she built a casserole of scalloped potatoes, which she put in the oven to bake, and prepared a pot of carrots that Cole and Tanner could simply turn on and cook. She put the second load of laundry in the dryer, made frosting for the cake and checked her watch. It was nearly noon. Where had the morning gone?

She fixed a plate of sandwiches and put it on the table, along with sliced pickles and a pitcher of water. Coffee was brewing and she was doing the dishes when she heard the mudroom door open and boots stomping on the mat.

The boys paused in their playing and looked at her as if to say, "What's that noise?"

Tanner came in first. Maddy hadn't seen Tanner in some time, but he looked the same as ever. A bit slighter than Cole, and a bit younger, with crinkles at the corners of his eyes that spoke of a devilish nature. He'd been a bit of a hellion in his younger years, though Maddy hadn't heard anything remarkable about him lately. Cole followed behind, tall, steady, a grown-up, serious version of his brother. Where Tanner's eyes had an impish gleam, Cole's held a certain warmth and steadfastness. Luke wobbled to his feet, tottered over to Tanner and lifted his arms. "Bup! Bup!"

Maddy laughed, and Cole spoke up. "Tanner, meet Luke."

"You got it right!" she praised. "You're a quick study."

Tanner reached down and picked up Luke, unfazed by the sight of kids in his home. "Hey, there." He settled the boy on his arm and looked at Maddy. "Nice to see you. Let me guess, this is your extrovert?"

She nodded. "Liam's my serious one." A quick glance showed Liam holding back, his eyes troubled. "He's more…reserved."

"Sounds like Cole and me," Tanner observed. "Here, partner. I'm gonna put you down now. Looks like your mama made lunch, and I need to wash up."

"Me, too," Cole said, a strange look on his face.

"Mum mum mum mum," Liam hummed after the men had gone to wash up. "Unh."

Maddy was looking forward to actual words. As it was she had to translate, and she knew what Liam wanted—his share of the attention, and something to eat. With a sigh, she put him on her hip, then dug in the diaper bag for a few small covered dishes. When Cole and Tanner returned, she was sitting at one end of the table, a boy on each knee, with a dazzling array of Cheerios, tiny cheese cubes and banana scattered on the surface.

She raised an eyebrow at Cole. "Now you see why I leave vacuuming for last."

He smiled warmly. "They'll learn table manners in time."

"I know. But I'm about to wear a fair bit of that banana. Those cute little hands will have it smeared all over my shirt in seconds."

Tanner took a chair. "This is great, Maddy. Thanks for making lunch."

"I hope it's okay. I wasn't sure how big a meal you ate at noon."

"This is fine," Cole said, reaching for a sandwich. "It's usually something like this, or some leftovers or something." He looked over at the counter. "Is that cake?"

"Yes, chocolate, with peanut butter frosting. For your sweet tooth." She smiled a little, teasing him.

"I should never have told you that."

"Well, you did. So now I know how to get around you. Just keep you flush with baked goods."

He pointed his sandwich at her. "You think it's that easy?"

They were openly teasing now, and she realized Tanner was looking from his brother to her and back again. Luke patted his hand against a beautifully soft circle of banana and Liam shoved three Cheerios awkwardly into his mouth.

Her smile faded a bit. "I'm not going to incriminate myself by answering that question. You are my boss, after all."

Tanner chuckled and reached for a few pickle slices. "Nice one."

The meal continued, but Maddy got the feeling Cole was put out about something. He didn't say much and there was a stubborn set to his mouth she hadn't seen before.

"I take it you boys can handle cooking some carrots

tonight? I have a ham in the slow cooker, and scalloped potatoes in the oven. All you need to do is heat up the potatoes and boil the carrots and you're done."

"Ham and potatoes? Damn, that sounds good." Tanner leaned back in his chair and stretched. "I'm going out, but I might just have to eat before I go if that's on the menu."

Same old Tanner. She looked over at Cole. He'd finished his meal and was wiping his fingers on a paper napkin. "Thank you, Maddy. That sounds terrific."

"You're welcome. I wasn't sure what clothes belonged to whom, so everything is folded and in the laundry basket. You and Tanner can sort it out."

"Sounds good."

Luke started to squirm on her knee while Liam still methodically ate Cheerios. Maddy realized she'd left hand wipes in the bag, and when she reached for a paper napkin to clean Luke's hands, all she did was smear the stickiness around.

Without a word, Cole got up, opened a drawer, took out a cloth and wet it at the sink.

"Here," he said quietly, handing it over.

She took it gratefully, surprised that she hadn't even had to ask. In a few quick movements she'd wiped both of Luke's hands and his face and put him down on the floor. He went into the living room, his tottering gait so typical of a child new to walking, and grabbed a stuffed cow that mooed when he shook it up and down. Which he did. Several times.

"Ooo. Ooo." Liam's attention was shot now, so she wiped him off and let him go, too.

Tanner got up from the table and took his plate to the dishwasher. "Hey, Cole, I'm going to run that errand we talked about earlier."

"Sounds good. I'll see you back here later."

"Thanks for lunch, Maddy." Tanner smiled and headed for the mudroom. "'Bye, boys," he called cheerfully.

"Tanner hasn't changed a bit, has he?"

Cole shook his head, a sheepish smile on his face. "Not much. Though he tends to be a little more discreet than he used to be. Thank the Lord for that."

Maddy had heard stories of how Tanner had gotten married in Vegas when he was younger, and that the marriage had only lasted a few days. But she wouldn't ask about that and she wouldn't judge. She knew how it felt to be on the receiving end of that sort of talk.

"He's just a bit reckless, that's all. But he's still young. Hell, he's only twenty-five."

She smiled. "And your thirty-three is so old."

"Older than your thirty-one."

A squeal and cry erupted from the living room and Maddy got up to sort it out. By the time she'd returned, Cole had cleared the table and loaded the dishwasher— including wiping the mess her sons had made on the kitchen table.

"That's supposed to be my job," she said.

"Whatever. It's nearly time for you to be off the clock, anyway."

"The boys have been really good," she said, turning back to the remaining bowls in the dishwater she'd left. It had cooled, but there was still hot water in the kettle and she added it to the sink. "They're going to get tired soon. One o'clock is a good quitting time."

He picked up a towel and started to dry the last of the dishes.

"Cole, I know you want to get back to work. Really, I've got this. You're set for today and I'll be back day after tomorrow. There should be ham left that you can have for tomorrow's dinner."

"Do you have to be so, I don't know, businesslike?"

There was an edge of irritation to his voice that surprised her. "Isn't that what I'm here for?"

He huffed out a breath. "It just feels weird." His gaze caught hers and the intensity of it made her catch her breath.

"If you didn't want me to work for you, you shouldn't have offered me the job."

He opened his mouth to say something, but then shut it again, as if he thought better of it. She narrowed her eyes. "What were you going to say just now?"

"Nothing. It's not important."

"Okay, then." The kids were tuning up again, starting to fuss as nap time neared. "I really want to run the vacuum over the floors, Cole. I'll see you Friday. Okay?"

But his eyes didn't let her go. They held her, tethered there, for long seconds while the boys played with toys, a whiny undertone to their chatter. For the briefest of moments he dropped his gaze to her lips and back up again. But it was long enough for heat to rise to her cheeks. The last thing she wanted to do was be bashful, to acknowledge such a small thing could affect her in any way. So she lifted her chin just a little and kept her shoulders straight.

Unless she was imagining things, there was a new light of respect in his eyes.

"I'll see you Friday," he said, stepping back and giving her a nod.

"Yes, and at the tree lighting, too," she added. "That's Friday night."

"Right."

And still he didn't leave…until the silence grew awkward.

"Well, 'bye." He smiled, a little uncertainly, and then went to the boys and knelt down. "'Bye, boys," he said. He held up a hand and Luke rushed forward and gave him a sloppy high five. Liam hung back and stared.

Cole looked over his shoulder at her. "He's going to be a tough one to win over."

And then finally, blessedly, he was gone to the mudroom. Maddy let out a breath and counted to ten, then busied herself around the kitchen and living room, picking up as much as she could so that they'd be ready to go once the floors were done. Once she heard the door slam behind Cole, she ventured into the mudroom and got the vacuum from the closet. She sat the boys on the sofa, and they were just tired enough they stayed put for the ten minutes it took her to finish tidying and put the vacuum away.

Then there were snowsuits and boots to put on and mittens and the trip to the car to fasten them inside and by the time Maddy was on the road back home she was exhausted. She really should do some baking for Sunday's coffee break after church, but she thought she just might have a nap instead when the boys were asleep. The idea sounded decadent and very, very lovely.

Instead the boys fussed and resisted being put down until, worn-out, they finally collapsed, sprawled on her bed so there was no room for her. She covered them with a blanket, then tiptoed down to the sofa to try to settle her frayed nerves. She was just drifting off, in a hazy half-conscious state and thinking about Cole's finely shaped lips, when the phone rang. And rang, and rang because she couldn't find the handset to the cordless. It went to her voice mail, but not before Liam woke up and started crying.

At that point Maddy felt a bit like crying herself.

She was just so completely overwhelmed. With everything. With handling it all on her own. Yes, she was still so incredibly angry and hurt by Gavin's deception. But most of all she missed him. After all he'd done, she still missed him, and his smile, and the way he'd take one of the boys and share the load with the kids and step in and cook dinner if she'd had a crazy day. Maybe his betrayal hurt all the more because in so many ways she'd thought they'd had a strong marriage. A partnership.

She missed his help, missed having someone to talk to at the end of the day, missed having someone to tuck her against his side in bed at night and make her feel secure and safe and not so damned alone. Even though things had been strained during the final months of their marriage, she'd thought they'd work through it. She'd thought it was just the adjustment to having twins and being parents and not having as much time for each other.

Tears were streaming down her face as she went to get Liam, who was snuffling and wiping his eyes with a fist. She took him downstairs so Luke could still sleep, and put him down before she sank into the couch cushions.

He was a year old, couldn't speak, didn't understand a bit of why she was upset. But at that moment, he patted her on her knee, lifted his arms for up, and when she picked him up and held him in her arms, he didn't fuss. He just snuggled in against her chest, tucked his face against the warm curve of her neck and put his pudgy little hand on her cheek.

"I love you, little man," she said softly, sinking back into the corner of the sofa and folding her legs yoga-style. She turned her head a little and kissed his soft hair, and he patted her cheek with his fingers, a move she knew he found consoling. Like a constant reassurance that she was there. Not going anywhere.

Five minutes later she stretched out her legs, slid down in the cushions and looked down at Liam's sleeping face.

Safe. Secure. Not alone.

She could provide that for her son. And she was living proof that she could make it on her own. But sometimes she wished someone was there to take away her loneliness, too.

Chapter Four

The Gibson Christmas tree lighting was a big event. In past years, it had been a simple one-hour community occasion that was decently attended. But this year, with the advent of Snowflake Days, it was bigger and better. As Maddy parked her car in the fire department lot, she was amazed at the crowd already gathered. The lighting wasn't for another forty minutes.

Her mom was in the passenger seat and her dad was squished in with the boys and their car seats in the back. "Are you guys okay with the stroller and stuff? I didn't think I'd be needed this early."

Her mom, Shirley, laughed. "Honey, the boys will be fine. We'll just sneak a little rum and nutmeg into their milk and…"

"Mom!"

Her dad's chuckle came from the back. "Maddy, you go. Leave us the keys, though, will you? So we can make sure we have everything and can lock it?"

She nodded and handed over the keys. "No candy canes for the boys, okay? I don't want them to choke."

She hopped out of the car and left the diaper bag behind for her parents. No candy canes? Ha. She'd learned one thing about grandparents very quickly. They nodded and agreed and then spoiled kids as soon as Mom's back was turned. Maddy reminded herself that her mom had raised three kids and they'd all survived. Besides, she was too grateful for the help to say much at all. Since her brothers both lived out of state, she figured that one day she'd be able to repay the favor when her parents got older and needed help.

Cole was at the food donation station already, and he looked up and smiled as she approached. "Hey, there," he greeted, and she couldn't help but smile. He was bundled up in a heavy jacket and boots and mittens, but wore a ridiculously plush Santa hat on his head. "Sorry I missed you at the house today. I had errands for the festival and didn't get back in time."

"It was no problem. I hope the chili was okay."

"It was perfect." He took a bag of food items from one family and thanked them. "Okay. So here's what I've done. Canned goods in one box, paper and cleaning items in another, pasta and rice and all the other stuff in this box. There are extra boxes under the table here if you need them." He grinned, showing his perfectly white teeth. "And by the looks of this crowd, you're gonna need them."

She'd been half happy, half disappointed Cole hadn't been at the house when she'd dropped by, and when Tanner had come in for lunch she'd kept busy making the chili while he ate rather than sitting and talking. And now she had this overjoyed feeling at seeing Cole again. She was a little embarrassed, bashful when their eyes met, a delicious twirly sensation tumbling in her stomach when she heard his deep voice. She surely wasn't ready to move on, so why did she constantly feel like a schoolgirl around Cole Hudson? She reminded herself that he tended to have this effect on girls. He always had, even when they were in school. And yet he'd never had the reputation of being a ladies' man. Not like his brother.

She stepped forward and accepted a grocery bag of donations from a family, finding an assortment of toothpaste, soap and shampoo inside. She put it in the proper box and jumped in surprise when she turned around and Cole put his Santa hat on her head.

"What are you doing?"

"Whoever works the station has to wear the hat," he decreed.

"I've got a knitted one," she protested, but then realized she'd left it in the diaper bag. With her parents.

"Is it invisible?" he asked.

She smiled at a teenage couple who came over, holding hands, and offered a jar of peanut butter and another of jelly. Cute.

"Don't you have somewhere to be?" she asked, annoyed. And amused, damn him. She let the hat sit atop her head where he'd awkwardly placed it.

"Sure do. I get to plug in the lights. Let's hope I don't have one of those Clark Griswold moments where I plug them in and nothing happens."

She did laugh at that. *Christmas Vacation* was one of her favorite holiday movies.

"I don't want to keep you. Maybe you'd better check

each one individually. And definitely make sure they're twinkling."

He leaned forward, a devilish look in his eye that made her realize that he and Tanner really did resemble each other. He touched the tip of her nose with his finger. "You are cheeky tonight," he said, and he winked at her. Winked! "I like it."

Her lips fell open and she scrambled for a crushing response, but before her brain kicked back into gear, he was gone.

The hat was warm from his head and she tucked it closer around her ears as the crowd grew and the food donation boxes filled. She greeted neighbors and friends, people she knew by sight but not by name by virtue of working in the library, and nearly everyone wished her a merry Christmas. The high school band teacher conducted a few instrument ensembles for background music, the trills of flutes and jazzy notes of saxophones brightening the air. Several feet away the business association, small though it was, had a table set up with cookies from the market and huge urns filled with hot chocolate and mulled cider. The rich, spicy scent was delicious.

At 7:00 p.m. sharp, Cole stood on a podium and got everyone's attention with a sharp whistle. "Merry Christmas, everyone!" he called out.

Holiday wishes were returned enthusiastically by the crowd, along with clapping.

"I don't have a microphone, so I'll keep this short and sweet. Welcome to Gibson's first ever Snowflake Days! Tonight we're going to light our tree and sing a few carols and have an all-around good time. Tomorrow there's a craft sale at the church, and you won't want to miss it. I heard Gilda Turner's made her famous fudge."

There were laughs through the crowd. Gilda was getting close to ninety and every boy and girl who'd grown up in Gibson had, at some point, tasted Gilda's fudge. There was none like it anywhere.

"And at the library tomorrow afternoon, we've got wagon rides for the kids, plus treats and story time. Finally, tomorrow night at the Silver Dollar, we have a dance for the grown-ups. Admission is ten dollars at the door and all the proceeds are going to the playground fund for a new structure to be built in the spring."

A round of clapping filled the air.

"Now," he said, his voice echoing over the crowd, "I'm going to turn things over to Ron here—" he nodded to his right "—and we can start the caroling. But first...can we have a drumroll, please?"

Maddy snorted, the scene from *Christmas Vacation* still in her head. Someone from the band did a roll on the snare and at the moment Cole went to plug the tree into the extension cord, he looked over in her direction, a goofy expression on his face. She half expected him to break out in "Joy to the World."

Then the tree was lit, all thirty feet of it, top to bottom in beautiful colored lights that reflected off the snowy evergreen tips. A collective *ooh* sounded, and then clapping, and then the choir director, Ron, took the podium and started the crowd singing "Santa Claus Is Coming to Town."

Cole jumped off the podium and disappeared into the crowd. Maddy let out a sigh and hummed along with the song. Donations had slowed to a now-and-again occasion, so she tidied the area and packed the boxes more efficiently for delivery. She half expected Cole to show up again, and when he didn't she pushed down the disappointment. She had no business looking for him. Sure, they'd seen a lot more of each other in the past few weeks, but she shouldn't make that into anything.

She had to worry about Liam and Luke, and that was all.

At eight o'clock she finally caught sight of him again, coming around the perimeter of the crowd. Things were wrapping up now; the crowd was down to about half, and the hot chocolate and cider were being packed up and the garbage put into bags. She hadn't even seen her parents or the boys, but she hadn't heard them fussing, either, so everything must have gone just fine.

"Wow, you've got everything ready to go," Cole remarked as he stepped up to the table. "Once the crowd disperses, I'll bring the truck down and we can put everything in the back."

"It was a good turnout, I think."

"I think so, too." He grinned at her. "I saw your mom and dad with the boys. They were sound asleep. The boys, I mean," he added, making her laugh.

"Fresh air and moving in the stroller will do that," she replied. "Unfortunately for me, that means they'll probably fight going to bed tonight."

"I never thought of that."

She raised an eyebrow. "Cole, there are many times that that's *all* I think about." She chuckled. "Sleep suddenly takes on a life of its own when you're not getting enough. Though to be honest, it's better now. They do sleep through the night. It's more getting them down at a decent time." Maddy put her hands into her jacket pockets, her fingers chilly despite the gloves she wore. "I find I like to have an hour or so to myself to unwind. To read a book or watch a movie uninterrupted."

"Maybe the boys can have a sleepover at your parents' place sometime."

She frowned. "Oh, Cole, I couldn't ask them to do that. They do so much already."

The caroling ended with a rousing version of "We Wish You a Merry Christmas" and then everyone headed for their cars, chatting and laughing. Maddy held the sound close to her heart. She loved living here. Loved the goodwill of the town, even despite the whispers she knew still happened behind hands. Eventually they'd forget, wouldn't they? Maybe, just maybe, if she found a way to let it go and move on, everyone else would, too.

She looked over at Cole. He didn't seem to care about the rumors at all. "Cole, can I ask you something?"

"Sure." White clouds formed from his breath as he looked over the crowd, lifting his hand in a wave at someone he knew.

"When Gavin…well, when it came out that Gavin had been seeing Laura, were you surprised?"

The question certainly surprised him. His gaze snapped to hers and his face flattened into a serious expression. "Wow. Okay. To be honest, yes, I was surprised. I thought you guys were solid. And Gavin never struck me as a cheater."

Tears stung her eyes. "Me, too. I think that's what

keeps me from moving on. How could I have been so wrong about him?"

"I don't know," he answered honestly.

"They dated in high school. You knew that, right? Maybe he never got over her."

"Have you asked her?"

Maddy's blood ran cold. "Of course not. I can't do that."

"I understand. She might be able to give you some answers, though. It might help."

"I…I just can't, Cole. It's too humiliating. Besides…" She looked up at him. He was watching her earnestly, as though he was really trying to help. It had been a long time since Maddy had truly felt as if someone was on her side. Most people were angry on her behalf, thinking they were being supportive. And they were…to a point. But this was different. This wasn't righteous indignation. It was genuinely trying to help her sort through her feelings, and she appreciated it the most out of all he'd done for her lately.

"Besides," she continued, "I'm not sure I want to know the details. I just want to find a way to let it go, so it doesn't matter anymore."

He lifted his gloved hand and put it on the side of her face. "You will," he said with a quiet confidence. "When the time is right, you will. You're a strong woman."

She suddenly felt like the Grinch, whose heart grew a few sizes. Hers felt warm and full as she looked into his face, illuminated by the light of hundreds of Christmas bulbs on the tree.

"Maddy, are you ready to go?" Her mother's voice came across the clear air and Maddy quickly stepped back and away from Cole's innocent touch. He dropped his hand and schooled his features quickly.

"I'll go get the truck," he said, and set off to the parking lot.

The stroller wheels squeaked on the snow as her parents approached. The twins were tucked in with blankets, sleeping peacefully. A tender feeling stole over Maddy as she looked down at them. Tired as she could be, and stressed with supporting the three of them, she loved them so much. There was nothing better than hearing their big baby belly laughs or getting sloppy kisses and warm cuddles.

"Cole's gone to get the truck. I wanted to help him put the boxes in the back before I took off."

"Cole, huh?" her dad asked, his blue eyes twinkling at her. "He's a nice guy."

"Yes, he is. And that's all he is, Dad."

"Well, shoot."

Her lips fell open. "I thought you always liked Gavin!" How could they be rooting for a new…whatever? Boyfriend? That sounded ludicrous.

"Honey, we did. We were so shocked when…well, you know. But you're too young to be alone."

"And it's too soon for me to be thinking of anything else," she reminded them. Gavin had been gone less than six months.

Cole's truck crept toward them and Maddy turned away from her parents, hoping they couldn't see her hot blush. Maybe she was reminding herself as much as them?

Cole hopped out and Tanner got out of the passenger side. "Hey, Maddy," he said easily. He gave a nod to her parents, shot a smile down at the sleeping boys and then, with the boundless energy he always seemed to have, let down the tailgate and reached for the first box.

"You probably want to get those boys home and out of the cold," Cole said, picking up a box. "I found Tanner, so there's no need for any help loading this up. We'll have it done in no time."

"You're sure?"

"I'm sure. Go home and have a glass of wine and I'll probably see you around tomorrow at some point. I'll be out and about at the different events."

"All right." She was tired, and tomorrow she wouldn't have any help with the boys. Hopefully they'd sit quietly while she was reading stories at the library. They did tend to love story time, thankfully.

They made their way back to the lot and Maddy's brow puckered in confusion. "I thought I parked over there?" she said, pointing at an empty area of the fire station lot.

"Your car's right there," her dad said, pointing to the right. "Long day, sweetheart?" His voice was teasing, but Maddy was certain she hadn't parked there.

"Do you have the keys, Dad?"

"Right here." He pulled them out of his pocket and handed them over.

As they approached her car she noticed something stuck under the windshield wiper. Closer examination showed it to be a promotional Christmas card from McNulty's Auto, just a few doors up the street. She took it from under the wiper, thinking it a simple holiday advertisement, but there was a piece of paper stapled to the top.

Merry Christmas, and drive safely—from Santa Claus. Then there was a receipt, rung up for zero dollars but showing four brand-new winter tires.

New tires?

She stepped back from the vehicle and looked down. Sure enough, there were brand-new tires on her car. It was exciting, on one hand, but on the other, she didn't like charity. "Dad? Did you and Mom do this?"

There was a gleam in her father's eye. "No, we didn't. Must've been Santa."

"Don't be ridiculous." She frowned. "And is this why my car was moved? You have to know something. You had the keys."

Her dad merely shrugged. "Maybe we should get the boys out of the cold?"

"Mom?"

Her mom, too, was trying hard not to smile but looking as pleased as the cat that got the cream. "It is chilly for them to be out so long."

She wasn't going to get anything out of her parents. She recognized the expression on their faces, and they could keep a secret like nobody's business.

The whole way back to her parents' place, Maddy wondered who would have gifted her with the tires. The only person she could think of was Cole, and that was a stretch at best. It was a long way from talking more often to spending hundreds of dollars for such a present. He was already helping her out by giving her the extra work. It couldn't be him.

Besides, he'd been at the tree lighting all evening, and it must have been a very fast job to get it done in the little over an hour she'd worked the food-bank booth. It had to have been her parents. It was a very nice, very practical Christmas gift.

"Thank you both," she said, once she'd pulled into their driveway. "I've been meaning to put tires on and should have done it weeks ago."

"Santa," her father reiterated with a grin. "Drive safely."

Drive safely. The same words as on the note. She had to admit, she was relieved. It was easier to accept such a thing from her parents than someone else.

Once she got home, she wrestled the boys inside, changed them into pajamas, gave them each a drink of warm milk and tucked them into bed, taking a few minutes to sing softly beside their cribs, hoping to soothe them back to sleep. It took about a half hour, but when they were finally asleep she sneaked out the door and let out a deep breath.

Cole's parting words echoed in her head. Feeling indulgent, she did just as he suggested. She poured herself a glass of wine, ran a hot bath and dug out the book she'd been reading about twenty pages at a time.

Maybe it was high time she started pampering herself a bit.

And if she thought about Cole Hudson while doing it, she wasn't going to beat herself up about it. She'd been a wife, a widow and the object of pity for too long. Maybe it was past time she felt like a woman again.

Chapter Five

Cole felt Tanner's eyes on him the whole way home.

"If you have something to say, just say it," Cole growled. Tanner was grinning at him like a fool and Cole wasn't in the mood.

He'd been thinking too much about Maddy's smile... and knowing he shouldn't be. That didn't fit in the category of "being neighborly."

"You are one sneaky bastard," Tanner finally said, leaning back in the seat and chuckling. "I wondered when you hired her to help out at the house. Hell, bro, we've managed on our own before for a few weeks."

"That's not it at all," Cole protested. "Gavin left her in a hell of a mess, and she's trying to make a Christmas for those boys."

"And the winter tires? You went to a lot of bother to have them put on without her knowing. Not to mention the expense."

"She's driving out to the ranch with just those all-seasons on. It's not safe."

"Sure."

Cole's annoyance grew, and he knew it was because

his brother was right. This did go beyond being good neighbors. But what did it mean? Or what did he want it to mean? "Look, let's just say I'm playing secret Santa for a family who could use a hand this Christmas, okay?"

"Sure," Tanner repeated, in that same smug, infuriating voice.

Cole glanced over at Tanner. "The committee for the festival has a list of families who applied for some help to get through the holidays. Know who's not on the list? That's because she's too damn proud. And I can't blame her. Her private life has been the topic of conversation around this town for the last half of the year, probably longer. I can't imagine she'd like her financial situation made public, too. She's a good person who got a raw deal and if you don't want to help, that's fine, but you can get off my case about it."

Tanner's teasing smile disappeared. "Damn, Cole, calm down. I was just riding you a bit. You don't usually give me ammunition. I was just having a little fun."

Cole sighed. "Look, I'm a bit touchy. Maddy's a nice woman. But people can be judgy."

"No judgment here." Tanner lifted a hand in peace-making gesture. "I'm the last person to pass judgment on anyone. If you want help, say the word. I like Maddy, too, and her boys are something."

They sure were. Busy and rambunctious when awake, but little angels when they slept.

Tanner lowered his hand and spoke again. "Just so we're clear, if you did happen to have feelings for

Maddy, I wouldn't say a word. Hell, it's the first time I've seen you fired up over a woman since—"

"Don't." Cole bit out the word. He didn't want to talk about Roni. He'd given her everything he had, and she'd cut and run, leaving nothing more than a note behind.

"Hey," Tanner said, quieter, "I like Maddy. She's always been real nice. My only caution would be to say you've got your work cut out for you. Can't imagine she's too fond of romance right now."

"You got that right." Cole tapped his hand on the steering wheel. "Which makes this a nonissue. Anyway, the only job I've got for you tomorrow is to give me a hand delivering all this to the food bank."

"You got it."

The cab of the truck was quiet for a while, and then Cole posed a question that had been on his mind for some time. "Hey, Tanner? You ever think of getting married again?"

Tanner laughed. "Again? I'm not sure three days in Vegas really constitutes being married in the first place. Legally? Yeah, I guess it was. But it wasn't like we, uh, had a marriage. It was a stupid idea and I'm not in any hurry to repeat it. If that answers your question."

"Sorta," Cole replied. But he wasn't going to pry further. Tanner had a right to his privacy, too.

The topic was completely dropped as they arrived home, locked the truck in the garage and headed inside where it was warm. But even as they sat down to watch TV, Cole couldn't get Maddy off his mind. The way she'd smiled up at him tonight had made his chest feel weird, as if it was expanding or something. He wished he could have seen her face when she realized she had four brand-new tires on her car.

He'd made her parents promise not to tell. He didn't want her knowing they came from him. But he wished he could have seen her smile anyway.

He could call himself Santa Claus or a good neighbor or however he wanted to put it. But Tanner had been closer to the truth.

Cole was getting sweet on Maddy Wallace, and he wasn't at all sure what he wanted to do about it—if anything.

SOMETIMES MADDY WISHED the boys were older so they could walk on their own and didn't always need to be in a stroller or in her arms. Of course, she reminded herself, that also meant that she'd end up having to chase them around. Still, as she carried a backpack with supplies and a kid on each arm, she felt like little more than a pack mule.

Snowflakes fluttered through the crisp air as she crossed the library parking lot to where a wagon and team of horses waited. Despite her weariness, she smiled at the sight of the wagon. Duke Duggan sat up front on a makeshift seat, holding the reins in his hands. The wagon's sides were decorated with swoops of red and green garland, and one of the horses stamped its feet, the sound of bells jingling through the air. Quinn Solomon was already seated with his daughter, Amber, and Rylan Duggan was waiting by a ramp that had been fashioned to help passengers aboard.

"Afternoon, Maddy." Rylan gave a roguish grin. "You and the boys goin' for a ride?"

"Apparently." She smiled back. "Where's Kailey today?"

"Working the craft show and lunch. She's handling the cash box for the raffle, and Lacey's at one of the bake tables." He gave a nod. "I don't remember anything like this from when I was a kid."

"Are you coming on the sleigh ride, too?"

He laughed. "Naw, I'll leave that up to Duke. I get to do crowd control."

She did laugh then. She'd just bet Rylan would be a great bouncer, but there wasn't a lot of need for muscle at a Christmas sleigh ride.

"Ma'am?" he said, holding out his hand.

"I got this," said a voice behind her, and a delicious shiver went down her spine. *Dammit.*

She schooled her features and turned around, pasting on a platonic smile that she hoped gave no hint of the sudden rapid beating of her heart. "Oh, hi, Cole."

"Hi." His smile warmed her clear through. "You've got your hands full, as usual." He reached out and took Liam into his arms, the movement looking strangely natural for a bachelor. Liam stared up at him with big blue eyes, most of his face shadowed by his thick hat and scarf.

"I thought I'd take the boys on the ride before story time," she said.

"That's a great idea. Let's get on and get good seats."

Let's? As in the both of them?

He gestured with his free hand and she had no choice but to go up the ramp ahead of him. Once on the wagon, she moved toward the front and perched on a bale of hay covered with a dark blue blanket. Quinn was across from her, listening to his daughter chatter on a mile a minute. Cole sat beside her and settled Liam on his knee. "So," he said conversationally, "did you enjoy the tree lighting last night?"

"I did. The committee did a great job."

"Are you going to the dance tonight?"

She laughed. "Right. I'll probably be in bed by nine o'clock. These guys went to sleep okay last night, but they got up at five."

"Don't you ever get to go out, Maddy?"

The question hurt a little. She and Gavin had gone out quite often before the boys had come along. Their social life had been part of a perfect marriage. The nights out had become more infrequent after the twins had been born. Now she was too tired to go out, and even if she did want to, it was hard to justify the extra expense.

Never mind the whole third-wheel thing.

"Oh, I go now and then." She offered another smile, though it was harder to keep it on her lips. Luke fussed in her arms, and she looked away from Cole and focused on making her son comfortable.

The wagon was filling up and happy kid chatter eliminated the need for more conversation. Within minutes Rylan secured the gate at the back and Duke clucked to the horses, setting the wagon in motion. The bells on the harnesses jingled merrily and the boys perked up, looking around as they sensed the movement and heard the noise. They moved through the end of the parking lot and over a little curb, then the twenty yards or so to the walkway that followed the river.

There was a skim of ice on the water, making it dark and still, though it wasn't quite frozen enough for skating yet. The recent snow clung to the branches on the trees, and the passengers were full of holiday spirit as they jingled their way west.

Someone started up a chorus of "Jingle Bells" and soon everyone was singing along—some definitely louder than others, a few slightly off-key but making up for it with enthusiasm. Beside Maddy, Cole's tentative baritone joined in. He kept Liam on his lap, and she relaxed quite a bit, seeing as the boys were content to babble along with the singing and were busy looking around them.

"This is really nice," she commented as the song ended and the wheels squeaked against the thin layer of snow on the path. "I'm glad we came."

"Me, too." Cole smiled down at her and she got that weird weightless feeling again. He was a friend. He was technically her employer. It wouldn't do to have a crush, would it?

She blinked, looking away from his gaze. That was silly. A woman her age—a widow—had no business getting a crush. Crushes were for teenagers.

A little voice intruded, though. She was only thirty-one. Not quite in her dotage yet—even if she did feel it most of the time.

"Hey, guess what happened last night?" she asked, changing the subject. "I got new tires. The note said from Santa, but I know it was my mom and dad."

His face lit up. "You did? That's great!"

"I've been meaning to put my old ones on. But one more winter would have been pushing it. It's really a godsend."

"That was really thoughtful of them." He shifted Liam on his knee, settling him more into the crook of his arm as the group started a rendition of "Frosty the Snowman."

She nodded. "I don't know what I would have done without them the last few months. They've stepped in so much. I feel guilty about it sometimes, but it's not forever."

"Your parents are great. I remember your dad keeping hard candies behind the counter at the hardware store. Whenever I went in with Dad, he'd sneak me one."

She laughed and bounced Luke up and down on her knee, as he was getting restless. "He still keeps them there. Make sure you ask him for one the next time you go in."

He laughed. "Pretty soon these guys will be asking him for candies. I'm sure your parents don't mind helping you, Maddy. According to my mom, grandkids are really important."

He said it with just a touch of acid in his voice, and Maddy laughed. "Getting pressure to settle down, are you?"

"Don't even." He lifted an eyebrow.

"Well, you are good with kids. I mean, the boys like you."

"They like Tanner, too." His eyebrow arched higher. "Though you can't fault a one-year-old for bad taste."

She giggled. "Funny. Tanner's…charming."

"And he knows it." Cole was grinning, too. "I shouldn't give him such a hard time. He's a good brother. A little… unreliable now and again, that's all."

Maddy sighed. "Aw, he's just not as weighed down with responsibility as some of us."

Cole shrugged. "Sometimes I wish I could be more like him."

Maddy thought for a minute. Yes, Tanner was charming, but she liked Cole's serious side. "You're fine the way you are, Cole."

His gaze touched hers, and she thought she saw a flicker of surprise in the depths. "What?" she asked. "Has no one told you that before?"

He shrugged. "Not really. Not that it's a big deal. I just… Oh, never mind. Let's start another carol."

He started everyone singing "Santa Claus Is Coming to Town," and Maddy marveled that he'd rather lead a carol in his tentative voice than talk about himself. Then again, guys weren't much into talking about feelings, were they?

She gave a derisive huff under her breath. Maybe if Gavin had talked about his real feelings earlier, he might not have felt the need to reconnect with his high school girlfriend.

They turned around at the other side of the bridge and started back toward the library, singing more carols and their breath forming clouds in the air. Liam was getting sleepy, and he cuddled into the lee of Cole's arm. Even Luke had mellowed out, resting his head against the chest of her puffy winter jacket. Cole looked over at her as they neared the parking lot. "God, they're sweet kids, Maddy. You're doing such a good job with them."

There was nothing he could have said that would have been a bigger compliment.

"You've held things together in a nasty situation," Cole said, his voice low so the rest of the people on the wagon wouldn't hear. "I know it can't be easy. I just… Don't let what happened make you feel bad about yourself."

She sighed. "I've tried over and over to figure out if I did something wrong, you know? I was so blindsided. I just can't figure it out. Maybe if I could, I'd stop being angry. Instead I feel…"

She stopped. This was more than she'd said to anyone before, even her parents. Certainly not her friends. She hadn't even asked if they'd known about the affair. She didn't want confirmation that she was the last to know.

"You feel what?" Cole leaned over a bit, his shoulder buffering hers a bit, creating a sense of intimacy.

She swallowed against a sudden lump in her throat. "Truthfully?" she murmured, her voice barely audible. "Stupid. I feel stupid."

He reached over with his free hand and squeezed her wrist. "You're not stupid."

"Whether I am or not is kind of irrelevant. I still feel like I am. It's like everything I thought I knew got turned upside down."

"Can I make a suggestion?"

"You're going to anyway, so go ahead." She aimed a lopsided smile at him.

He squeezed her arm again. "Don't be so hard on yourself."

She laughed. "That's it?"

"That's it." He gave a small nod. "Truth is, Maddy, if Gavin didn't want you to know, he would have hid things from you, so how were you supposed to figure it out?"

"Shouldn't I have seen the signs?"

Cole's gaze softened. "Honey, you trusted him and you believed in him. That says a lot about the kind of person you are."

"Gullible." She rolled her eyes.

"Kind," he contradicted. "Someone who looks for the best in people. More people should be like you."

He shifted Liam just a little, adjusting his weight as the boy's eyes grew heavy. "Like I said, your boys are lucky to have you."

His words sent a warmth through her, a confidence that she hadn't felt in many months. She tried to be a good mom, and she tried to stay positive. Maybe Cole was right. Maybe she should stop feeling foolish and stupid and just…move on.

It wouldn't be that easy, of course, but she had to stop looking for what she'd done wrong. It really didn't matter anymore, did it?

The horse team plodded into the library parking lot, bells still jingling. Maddy checked her watch and saw that it was 2:40, perfect timing for returning and getting everything set up for story time. Rylan was waiting in the parking lot and released the gate on the wagon, helping rosy-cheeked children disembark. Cole and Maddy were nearly last, since they were sitting up front, and Cole kept Liam in his arms.

"Thanks for your help, Cole. I'd better get inside."

"I'll help. After that I could use some hot chocolate."

"Cole, I can manage. If this is a veiled way of trying to give me a hand, I've been managing the twins on my own for a while now."

"Maybe I want to spend more time with you."

The words were such a surprise that she had no response. Her cheeks felt hot despite the bite in the air and she kept her feet moving toward the library doors. Up until now Cole hadn't actually come out and said that he was putting himself in her path. But what he'd just admitted was pretty clear, wasn't it?

And now she didn't really have time to decide how she felt about it. The crowd at the library was growing, she had a sneaking suspicion that the boys needed a diaper change, and she needed to take a breath before sitting down to entertain a bunch of kids.

Once inside she wordlessly took Liam from Cole's arms. He fussed a bit but she bounced him on her elbow and got him into better position before heading straight for the bathroom. Once both boys were taken care of, she made her way through to the reading corner at the back. It was decorated for the occasion, with a little artificial tree and twinkly lights. There was a rocking chair at the center, where she'd sit while reading, and several little cushions scattered around the carpet, waiting for children to get comfortable. A table was stationed nearer the entrance, where the floor wasn't carpeted, and Maddy saw hot chocolate being ladled out and cookies being consumed in huge quantities. Her stomach rumbled, but right now she hoped to sneak a few minutes to feed the boys so they'd be content during story time.

Maddy retrieved their sippy cups from her pack and sat one child on each knee, rocking in the chair as they gripped the cups in their chubby hands and drank away. She would have killed for a shortbread cookie or two—she'd missed lunch—but she was accustomed to waiting. Luke squirmed a bit to get settled, and more than a little milk dribbled down his chin, but Liam cuddled in like an angel.

Cole was over by the table, a cup of cocoa in hand, smiling and chatting with Pauline, who was jotting something down on a pad of paper as they spoke. Her heart gave a little stutter just seeing him there. Clearly he'd seen her reaction when he'd said he wanted to spend time with her and was giving her some space. Maybe she should have been cool about it, but this wasn't the same as before. Before, they'd run into each other by accident. Or she'd been at his house because he'd hired her...

She heard his laugh, singling it out from the other noise in the room. Who was she kidding? The job offer had been thinly veiled at best. It had just been easier to excuse away. Now, though, it seemed he was seeking her out.

She should probably just back away. He had no idea what he was getting himself into. She was an emotional wreck at best, exhausted all the time, and a good day was one where she didn't have evidence of motherhood

smushed into her shirt. She came as a total package…
and one that wasn't gift wrapped with a big bow, either.

She was messy. And altogether unsure if she was
really, truly interested.

Luke had stopped squirming and when she looked
down, she saw his eyelashes lying against his cheeks.
A wave of tenderness washed over her. Her precocious
one played hard and slept hard, and right now he looked
like an angel.

Eloise Parker, Maddy's boss, picked her way through
the crowd collecting on the carpet. "Looks like you're
going to have a full house," she remarked, smiling down
at Maddy.

"This should be easier with the boys settled down,"
Maddy agreed. "Believe me, I'm getting used to reading with a kid on each knee."

"You know I have spare arms. And it's been a while
since I've had a chance to cuddle my favorite boys."
Eloise looked down at the twins, her expression soft.
"With mine in college now, it seems forever since I
had small ones. And it'll be a few more years before
we have grandkids."

Maddy smiled back. El was such a wonderful boss.
Since Gavin's death, she'd been more than accommodat-
ing with the scheduling and Maddy's child-care quanda-
ries. It was another reason why Maddy couldn't imagine
leaving Gibson behind.

"Maybe just Luke?" Maddy shifted in her seat a little. "He's down for the count, I think. Liam's not quite
there yet."

"He won't wake up?"

Maddy shook her head. "Reach into the bag. There's a little blanket there. If you put it over him, he should stay asleep for a good half hour or more. But only if you have time, El. I know it's a busy day."

"Aw, I just came in to supervise. I'm doing more enjoying than working. It's fine." She grabbed the blanket from the pack, then carefully extricated Luke from Maddy's arms. With barely a snuffle, he nuzzled into her shoulder. She covered him with the soft fleece and he didn't stir.

That left Liam, and he was still taking the odd drink from his sippy cup. Eloise moved away with Luke, and with only one child on her lap Maddy was free to pick up the storybooks she'd requested.

"Good afternoon, everyone," she said in a clear voice.

"Good afternoon, Miz Wallace," the kids chorused, and Maddy grinned. Oh, goodness, this felt just like years in the past when she'd sat on the story mat in her elementary school library. Only then she'd been the child and she'd looked up at the librarian as if she were some sort of superhero.

Even then she'd loved the library. It wasn't much wonder she'd chosen this as her profession.

"Did everyone enjoy the sleigh ride?"

There was a chorus of chatter and Maddy grinned at the excitement. She looked for Cole but couldn't see him anywhere. Disappointment weighed surprisingly heavy, but she pushed it aside. The next half hour was all about the kids, anyway.

She picked up a book and opened it to the first page. "We're going to start with a few special stories today.

This first one is a real favorite of mine." She looked down at the beautiful illustrations. "*The Polar Express*, by Chris Van Allsburg."

The room quieted and she began to read. By the time she turned the first page, the audience was rapt.

She read about the adventures to the North Pole, the train, the special gift from Santa. And when that one was done, she picked up the second book: *How the Grinch Stole Christmas*.

As she made her way through it and the tongue-twisting words, Liam was also sound asleep, his tiny head drooped on her shoulder. She smiled down at the children. "Should I read one more?" she asked, knowing full well what the answer would be.

Once more there was a chorus of tiny voices urging her to continue. She looked up and saw Eloise sitting in a comfy chair, Luke still conked out. She picked up the book she'd been saving for last, trying not to notice Cole's absence but noting it anyway.

"'Twas the night before Christmas,'" she began softly, "'and all through the house, not a creature was stirring. Not even a mouse.'"

A little girl in the front, who'd been a little antsy through the other stories, bounced up and down on her bum, her hand in the air. "I know, I know!" she said loudly. "The sthockingth were hung by the chimbley!"

Maddy tried not to laugh. "That's right. But we need to try really hard not to interrupt, right?"

"Thorry, Mith Wallash."

The lisp was too adorable for words. The girl couldn't

be more than four, with strawberry blond pigtails and big blue eyes.

"Thank you, Darcy. Now, where were we? 'The stockings were hung by the chimney with care, in hopes that St. Nicholas soon would be there.'"

Another hand shot up and Maddy figured the attention span that had carried them through the first two stories was starting to waver. "Yes, Nathan?"

"Why is it St. Nicholas and not Santa Claus?"

Rather than get into the whole folklore, Maddy opened her mouth to explain when Bobby Rathbone called out, "Haven't you seen *The Santa Clause*? He has a whole lot of names besides Santa."

Maddy leaned forward a bit. "Boys and girls, how about we save our questions for the very end, okay?"

All faces turned to her again and she continued, grateful that the story wasn't too long, and putting lots of expression into the words.

When it was over, she closed the book and put it down by her side. "Thank you, everyone, for being such a wonderful audience. I hope you all have a merry Christmas, and make sure you write your letters to Santa so he knows what to bring you under your tree."

"Why write a letter when I'm right here?" came a booming voice, and Maddy looked up, startled, to see Cole's twinkling eyes staring at her from within a white bearded face and a hugely padded belly.

Oh, my sweet Lord. How on earth was she supposed to keep her distance from Santa Claus?

Chapter Six

"Santa!" The library echoed with excited screams, mingled with Cole's robust "Ho, ho, ho!" Liam's eyelids fluttered open at the chaos, but he didn't wake all the way. Maddy got up from her chair, more flustered than she cared to admit. "Santa, would you like my chair?" she asked.

"Why, thank you, Ms. Maddy. I'm mighty tired from my trip and could use a sit-down." He winked at her and she willed herself not to blush—and failed. Even in the ridiculous suit with all the padding, he was remarkably handsome.

He plopped himself down in the rocking chair and put his big red sack on the floor beside him. "Well, what have we here? I heard there was a special group of children here today. Did everyone like Ms. Maddy's stories?" Cole made his voice deep and jolly.

"Yeah!"

Maddy couldn't stop the smile that curved her lips. He was such a natural. So willing to step in and help out with whatever needed doing. Now she knew where he'd disappeared to. He'd gone to get into the Santa suit. Wasn't he just full of surprises?

"Now," he cautioned, leaning forward in the rocking chair and adopting a serious expression, "since today isn't actually Christmas Day, whatever is in my sack is just a little something fun. The elves are still working to have all the presents ready to deliver on Christmas Eve. Santa's pretty good with names, so when I call yours, come on up and tell me what you want for Christmas and get your gift."

Every eye in the place was glued to Santa's face as he reached into his sack. He held up a little package. "Ho, ho, ho! Says here this one is for Dillon Graves," he called out, and a little boy of about five or six came forward.

"That's me."

"Come on up here and tell Santa what you'd like for Christmas."

Dillon was a bit shy, but he came forward anyway, sat on Cole's knee and confessed he wanted a new Lego kit and a belt buckle like his uncle Gary's. Cole gave him his present and picked out the next package. "Let me see. This one is for Darcy McTavish."

The strawberry blonde with the lisp. Maddy hid her smile behind her hand as the girl rushed forward, her pigtails bouncing. "That'th me, Thanta!"

Even Cole struggled to keep a straight face. "Of course it is!" He patted his knee. "What would you like for Christmas, Darcy?"

And so it went, through twenty or more kids, each one taking a turn and accepting their token gift. The sound of ripping paper filled the air, and Maddy could see that each child got something fun and holiday themed—a make-an-ornament kit, or a Christmas activity book and markers—as well as a treat like a candy-cane reindeer or a gingerbread cookie. It had taken plenty of planning to add this to the afternoon's agenda, and a rush job, she suspected, to add names to each package so that there was one for each child.

Maddy had had no idea this was even part of the plan, but it was the perfect ending to the afternoon activity. When every child had received something, Santa bade the group farewell and disappeared out the library's main doors. Maddy wondered where his clothing was stashed, but she didn't have time to think about it much since Liam woke up and, being refreshed, squirmed to be put down.

It gave Maddy a few quick moments to pack up her stuff and help tidy the story corner, as well as grab a couple of cookies from the table. During all the commotion she'd forgotten about the hollow feeling in her belly, but now it was nearly four o'clock and she was starving.

By the time she had the boys straightened away and ready to go, the crowd had thinned out considerably. Dog tired now, Maddy herded them toward the car, wondering if she dared splurge on some takeout just this once. If she got fried chicken from the diner, she could share the fries with the boys and have a piece of chicken or two left for her dinner tomorrow.

"Maddy! Hey, Maddy, wait up!"

She turned around and saw Cole jogging toward them. *Maybe I want to spend more time with you*, he'd said. Her pulse did a little leap.

She looked up into his face as he drew near. His

chin was red, presumably from where he'd removed the white beard, but his eyes were as twinkly as when he'd sat in the chair and pretended he'd just arrived from the North Pole.

How did a person manage to be so…happy?

"Looks like we both had a busy afternoon," she commented lightly. "You're a man of many talents."

"I've never been so scared in all my life," he admitted, stopping in front of her. He must have washed his face and gotten some water on his hair, because his hairline was turning frosty white in the cold air. "I kept thinking one of those kids would recognize my voice or something or say that I was too young to be Santa. Or that my beard was fake and know that I had a pillow stuck in the suit."

Maddy laughed again. She seemed to do that with alarming regularity when Cole was around. "Most people believe what they want to believe. Kids included."

Once the words were out, she considered them. She'd said them off-the-cuff, but now they rang with truth. She was as guilty of it as anyone, wasn't she? Believing what she wanted to?

"So what are you doing now?" Cole asked, interrupting her thoughts.

"Oh, just getting the boys home, I guess. I thought about stopping at the diner for some supper. I'm not sure I feel like cooking tonight."

"Me, either," he said, putting his hands in his jacket pockets. "It's Saturday night, so Tanner's probably taken off to the city for the evening." Cole's eyebrow took on an arch that Maddy figured was the equivalent of rolling his eyes. "Guess I'll just be sitting home flipping through channels, with a sandwich for company."

This was leading somewhere, Maddy could feel it. And she welcomed it, though she wasn't about to take the reins.

Luke twisted around in her arms, restless with being held so long. "Sorry," she said, turning to open the car door. Cole reached around her for the door handle and opened it, and she put Luke into one seat and with one hand snapped the buckle into place. Then she went around to the other side and put Liam in his seat.

"Everything takes twice as long, huh?" Cole asked as she straightened and shut the door.

"You get used to it." She shrugged. "One of the girls at day care has three under five. That's two car seats and a booster seat. Besides, it won't be long and they'll be older and able to hop in themselves and all I'll have to do is buckle them in." And boy, was she looking forward to that.

"So, getting back to boring Saturday nights...why don't I pick up dinner and you take the boys home and I'll meet you there? It's got to be better than both of us eating alone, right?"

She hesitated, wondering if she should just ask the question on her mind. Was there any point in dancing around it? She'd always been a straightforward kind of person. "Cole, are you asking me on a date?"

His blue gaze held hers. "Well, technically, going out on a date would mean we actually, you know, went out somewhere."

He was skirting the topic. "Untechnically, then?"

"Is *untechnically* a word?"

"Cole." She said it meaningfully and his lips quirked.

"Okay. So if I said yes, that this was a date, would it change your answer?"

The idea of sharing a meal with him, with a grown-up…sounded lovely. And she needed to keep this in perspective. It was just a date. It wasn't as if he was proposing marriage or anything. Now that *would* be foolish.

"No."

"No is your answer? Or no, it wouldn't change it?"

She couldn't help it—she chuckled. "Are you being this way deliberately?"

He took a step closer to her. Her pulse leaped again. "It depends. Do you find it annoying or endearing?"

He looked so cute and hopeful she lost all her will-power. "Fried chicken. And I like extra coleslaw."

His answering grin lit his face, making him look boyish. How could a woman stay immune to that? Besides, he didn't know what he was getting into. The boys were terribly messy eaters. Cole was bound to get food on him somewhere.

"Great. I'll see you in half an hour or so?"

Half an hour. It might give her enough time to get home, do a quick five-minute tidy and freshen up. Because this was a date. No matter how they twisted the circumstances, no matter how casual…this was Maddy's first date since she'd become single again.

Holy crap.

"I'd better get going, then," she said, feeling a little breathless. "The boys hate sitting in their seats if we're not going anywhere." As if on cue, Luke started fussing, loud enough they could hear him through the closed windows. "Wait. Do you know how to get to my place?"

"It's on Oakleaf, right?"

She nodded, wondering how he knew that.

"See you soon," Cole called before she could ask, and with a parting smile, he turned around and headed across the lot for his truck.

Maddy got behind the wheel and took a deep, fortifying breath. Once she started the car, got the heater going and put it in drive, Luke quieted. And it was a good thing, because in her head she kept hearing the words *I have a date. I have a date. I have a date...*

The drive took ten minutes, and by the time she got home she wasn't sure if she was excited or nervous or both. So her frayed nerves really weren't prepared for what she found on her front doorstep.

A Christmas tree. A beautiful, full spruce that stood about seven feet tall, just tall enough to fit in her living room and put the angel on top without hitting the ceiling. A white tag fluttered in the wind.

She took both boys inside and deposited them in the living room on their play blanket surrounded by toys. Happy to be free to do as they pleased, both started pulling toys from the big yellow tub in the corner. Maddy stepped back outside and looked at the tag. *To the Wallace family. From your secret Santa.*

First the tires, and now a tree. Had her dad delivered it this afternoon? God bless him. Her parents had to know that Christmas was particularly difficult this year, and she loved how they were trying to make it better. She'd have to call them later and thank them. But right now Maddy worried more about the state of the kitchen and bathroom. Tomorrow would be time enough to dig out the decorations and the stand and have a go at the tree.

The surprise tree put her in an extrafestive mood, though, and she hummed as she put the dishes from the sink into the dishwasher and hurriedly wiped off the countertops. The pile of clean sippy cups in the drying rack got put away in the cupboard, and she hung the dish towel over the handle of the oven door instead of leaving it in a crumple. Then it was off to the bathroom to pick up dirty pajamas, give the sink a wipe and tidy the vanity.

A quick check on the boys and then she was zooming off to the bedroom. She hesitated, then pushed away the idea that Cole would ever see the inside of this room. She peeled off her sweater and put on a new one, a light blue one with a soft cowl neck. Her hair was a staticky mess from being under her hat. She dragged a brush through it and frowned. It needed…something. She tried a ponytail—too casual. Leaving it down—too limp. Up in a bun—too uptight. In the end she grabbed a thin white headband and slid it behind her ears. Hair down was good, and off her face made her feel less straggly.

Makeup. Maddy was well and truly flustered now, wanting to look nice but not wanting to look as though she'd put in a lot of effort and give Cole the wrong idea…or the right one, as the case might be. A quick reapplication of mascara and some tinted gloss brightened her eyes and lips without being overdone, and she left on the same jeans she'd worn to the library.

She shut the door to her bedroom as she left, then stepped into the boys' room and made a mad dash through the clutter, throwing dirty clothes in their hamper, straightening the bedding and dumping the diaper pail into the garbage in the garage.

It had taken her exactly fifteen minutes.

"Mama! Mama!"

Back in the living room, Liam was bobbing up and down, holding a fabric book in his chubby hand. "Mama," he said, one of the few words he could manage at only a year old. He waved the book in the air.

Luke had a plastic truck and was on his hands and knees, making *vroom* noises as he ran it over the carpet.

Cole's truck was pulling into the driveway.

Oh, Lord, oh, Lord, oh, Lord, she thought.

"Boys, how about some supper? Are you hungry?"

That got their attention. Luke's truck zoomed off course and careened into a chair; Liam dropped the book and Maddy tried to hold her composure as Cole got out of his vehicle carrying two paper bags.

He had no idea what he was walking into. And the trouble was, neither did she. And what freaked her out the most was realizing she desperately wanted to find out.

COLE CLUTCHED THE paper bags as if his life depended on it. The cashier at the diner had folded them over neatly and stapled the tops, but his death grip had crumpled them completely. A date. With Maddy Wallace.

With Maddy Wallace and her children, he reminded himself. But instead of making him feel better, his stomach tied up in even more knots. He was smart enough to know that when you dated a woman with kids, you dated the whole package. In the past few weeks he'd somehow gone from wanting to lend a helping hand to a neighbor to wanting to do a lot of things that weren't neighborly at all. And over it all was the sinking feeling that he'd been here before—that he was a fool to even think she'd want him.

The tree he'd had Tanner deliver was propped up outside the door, he'd noticed. Tanner had done a great job, too. The tree looked green and full and the perfect height. And Maddy would never suspect him as being her secret Santa, because he'd been at the library with her all afternoon.

He'd thought to take a moment to gather his wits before ringing the bell, but Maddy opened the door and smiled at him. Holy doodle, she looked good. If his memory served, she'd changed into different clothes from this afternoon, and her hair fell in silky waves to her shoulders. Her eyes were incredibly blue, her cheeks bright in a porcelain face, and her lips were pink and puffy and begging to be kissed.

And all around him was the scent of fried chicken, pulling him back to reality. God, he had to get a grip.

"Take-out delivery," he announced and held up the bags.

"Come on in." She stepped aside, making room for him to enter.

The first thing he noticed was how lived-in her house

looked. Not in a bad way, but in a cozy kids-live-here way that made him instantly comfortable. He thought of his great-aunt Gertrude's from when he'd been a boy. No one was allowed to touch her knickknacks, and they'd gotten in trouble for sliding in sock feet on her perfectly polished hardwood floor. Maddy's house was comfortable, with a chocolate-brown corduroy sofa and chair, beige carpeting, and a wooden entertainment unit with rounded corners. The boys ran around, but their toys were centered on a large colorful blanket on one side of the room.

"Excuse the mess," she apologized. "It's impossible to keep the place neat with two tornadoes blowing through at any given moment."

"It's great," he commented. "And perfect for a family." He handed her the bags and unzipped his jacket. "Know what I like about your kids, Maddy?"

"What?"

He took off his jacket and hung it on a hook beside the door. "They're happy. It wouldn't be right to bring them up in a museum where they couldn't touch anything, you know?"

"Well, what you see is what you get around here." She smiled. "Take off your boots and come into the kitchen. I've got to get a few things ready for the boys."

He put his boots on the mat and followed her into the kitchen. "I see you got a Christmas tree," he commented lightly, stepping into the brightly lit kitchen. Her comment about the tires earlier told him she didn't suspect, and it was kind of fun playing along.

"It must be from my dad. He's been doing this secret Santa thing this year. First the new tires on my car, then the tree." She got plates out of the cupboard, turned around and smiled. "I think they knew that Christmas spirit was in short supply this year and they're trying to do something fun."

Well, the motive was bang on, but the identity was all wrong. It was what Cole wanted—anonymity—but he felt a little bit jealous knowing she thought her father was responsible. Still, telling her up front would have just made her refuse. He could live without taking credit. He wasn't doing it for gratitude, after all. He just wanted to help, and he was in a position to do it.

"It was here when I got home this afternoon," Maddy continued, putting a dish in the microwave. "I'll have to search the basement for the tree decorations and stuff. Maybe I'll put it up tomorrow."

Cole went to the table and started taking takeout containers from the bags. "I suppose the twins don't remember last Christmas."

She shook her head. "Not hardly. They were so little." She took the dish from the microwave and tested the food inside with her finger. "Yummy, right?" She sent him a goofy smile. "They only have a few teeth, so I still have to keep things pretty mashed up for them. I'll feed them some carrots and peas and chicken, and then they can pick at cut-up fries while we eat. Hope that's okay."

Cole watched the process, intrigued.

Maddy had two small bowls, each with a rubber-tipped spoon. The boys were seated in high chairs, bibs over their clothes, excited that they were about to eat. Cole chuckled as Maddy filled the spoon for Liam, touched it to her lip to test the temperature and then moved the spoon in his direction. Just like a baby bird, he opened his mouth wide, very ready to eat.

She managed two spoonfuls before Luke demanded his turn by banging his hands on his high-chair tray. Calmly, Maddy put down Liam's bowl and picked up Luke's, repeated the process, and started to go back and forth.

Twins, Cole thought, and not for the first time, were a lot of work.

"Um, maybe I could try? That way you won't have to go between them."

Maddy looked up at him, her face blank with surprise. "You? Want to try feeding one of the boys? Have you ever fed a baby before, Cole?"

"How hard can it be?" He'd watched her. Food on spoon, spoon in mouth, repeat.

She laughed. "All right. Here, you take Luke's bowl. Not too fast."

"I got this." He pulled up a chair and took the bowl from her. Put some mushy green peas on the spoon and held it to Luke's mouth. As predicted, Luke opened wide and took the peas in one gulp. Cole looked over at Maddy and smiled widely. "See?"

"You're a pro," she replied, a silly smile on her lips. He liked seeing her smile, he realized. She looked so young and pretty when she did that.

He scooped up more food and sent it Luke's way. He soon realized that Luke wasn't as fond of the ground-up chicken as he was of the vegetables. Luke grabbed the spoon with a chubby hand and started pulling on it with surprising strength. "Come on, open up for chicken," Cole urged him, but Luke just moved his fist up and down until he suddenly let go—and the chicken on the spoon went flying. Straight onto Cole's shirt.

He heard Maddy snicker, but he refused to look at her. It was just a little chicken. He'd had far worse on his clothes.

"Put the chicken on first," she suggested quietly, "and then put the vegetables on over top. You have to be tricky sometimes."

Cole did what she suggested and Luke opened up immediately. Scamp.

They continued feeding the boys, who seemed to be big eaters considering the amount of pureed food they ate. "Do you make all your own food?" Cole asked, scraping along the side of the bowl.

"They're eating more table food now, being a year old," she commented. "But yeah. I make my own. Usually on a Saturday I'll cook stuff up, puree it in my little blender and freeze it in ice cube trays. Then I just pop them in a dish or baggie and they're good to go."

"Smart."

"Cheap. Cheaper than buying the bottled stuff. And now I can get by with just mashing it if it's smooth enough."

Cole looked over. "And better for them, too, right?" He kept the spoon moving, the last few mouthfuls accepted eagerly by Luke. "You're a good mom, Maddy."

"Thanks." She smiled sweetly, and he felt something warm and pleasant infuse him. "Um, you might want to slow down, though."

"What?" He looked at Luke. The poor kid's cheeks were puffed out with food. Cole had been so focused on Maddy that he'd just kept mindlessly shoveling it in.

"Oops," he said, sitting back. "Sorry, buddy."

Luke began to cough. And cough some more. And then his little blue eyes watered and he gave a big cough and…

Cole added carrots and peas to the chicken on his shirt.

There was stunned silence for a minute, and then Maddy started to giggle. And giggle. And before he could help himself, Cole was laughing back until the kitchen rang with their laughter and the sound of babies thumping their fists on their high chairs.

It was definitely the strangest first date he'd ever been on.

Maddy wiped her eyes on her sleeve. "Oh, gosh. I'm sorry. You just… Oh, you were so sure of yourself. And now you've truly been initiated."

"You warned me they were messy. I forgot." He grinned, grabbed a paper napkin from the takeout bag and dabbed at the mess on his chest and sleeves.

"You wait." She picked up the bowls and went to the sink. "Now I let them feed themselves. Sometimes I think I need to get a dog so it can do floor cleanup."

He chuckled. "It really is an adventure, isn't it?"

She shrugged. "It just is what it is. Come on, let's eat. I'm hungry."

Together they unpacked the chicken and fries and the large container of coleslaw, just as she'd requested. He'd added a couple of sodas to the order, too. "Wow, I think I must really be impressing you with the fine dining on this date," he joked, watching as she cut up a few handfuls of fries and put them on the trays for the boys.

"Were you trying to impress me?" she asked, and that little nervous bubble started rolling around in his stomach again. He hadn't dated in a long time. Hadn't felt like it. But Maddy had definitely captured his interest.

"Honestly?" He met her gaze. "Not really. I get the feeling if I tried to impress you, you'd see right through me."

Her smile faded. "I know. I'm cynical. It was much nicer when I was naive and oblivious."

She looked so down that he reached over and put his hand over hers. Hers was much smaller than his, and softer. "Maddy," he said quietly, "you are way too hard on yourself. And far from being oblivious."

"This is my first date since Gavin," she admitted, looking away.

"I know," he answered, a lump forming in his throat. "And it must seem strange. It's kind of why I wanted to keep it low-key. I get it. I get that you're scared and I get that the boys come first." He squeezed her fingers. "Maddy, look at me."

She looked up. Her eyes were wide and glistened a little. The lump in his throat grew bigger. For a moment Cole considered Gavin Wallace and felt the urge to put his fist through the other man's face simply because he'd hurt her this badly. Of course, that could never happen.

"We can go as slow as you need," he assured her. Beside them the twins made babbling noises as they played with their fries, but Cole kept his eyes locked with hers. "I like you. I like hanging out with you. It can be as simple as that, okay?" He wasn't sure he was ready for more than that, either. Being with her brought back all kinds of memories—good and bad. The wonder of being in love, tempered by the frustration at wanting to help and not getting through. Shit, he'd figured it was ancient history. Maybe he hadn't moved on as much as he'd thought.

She nodded. "I'm sorry for being such a downer."

He smiled a little, knowing if she could read his mind she'd see he was being the killjoy. "Seriously, if you apologize one more time…"

"Sorry," she said, and then put her fingers to her lips and smiled a bit.

"The chicken's getting cold. Let's just eat and take it from there, okay?"

"Okay," she agreed.

He slid his fingers off hers, and they relaxed a bit, biting into the crispy chicken and dipping fries in ketchup. She hadn't been kidding when she'd said she liked the slaw, because Cole watched as she used a fork to dump half the container on her plate.

When the meal ended, Cole took the dishes to the dishwasher while Maddy wiped sticky hands, let the boys out of their chairs and went to work wiping the trays and sweeping the mess off the floor.

As Cole collected the garbage from their meal and took it to the trash can, he realized how incredibly domestic it all felt.

And how he really didn't mind it at all.

Chapter Seven

Bath time was the perfect excuse for Maddy to get some breathing space. The boys were splashing happily while she knelt before the tub, making sure no one slipped. She grinned as Liam's hand smacked the surface of the water, making a loud slap noise and sending water everywhere. He looked so proud of himself.

And Cole was out in the living room. She'd been so surprised when he'd asked to feed Luke, and their shared laughter had felt wonderful for her soul. Oh, she'd missed that sort of scene so terribly. It might have made things simpler if Cole weren't good with the boys, or if he tried to exclude them from stuff. But he didn't. He dived right in and appeared to enjoy it.

Being good to her kids carried a lot of weight.

But the part that stuck in her mind the most was how he'd put his hand over hers and told her they could go as slow as she wanted. That courtesy and understanding had had the opposite effect, actually. Instead of being relieved and taking things back a notch, Maddy found herself wanting to turn her hand over and link her fingers with his. Found herself focusing far too much on the shape of his lips and wondering what it would be like to kiss him.

Oh, she was interested, all right. But she didn't really want to be. She wasn't sure she was ready yet, and Cole was too nice a guy to mess around with.

Still, she reasoned, he was a big boy. And she'd been very up-front with her feelings. If he asked her on another date…perhaps on a real date…she'd be tempted to say yes. The one thing holding her back would be what people would say. She was so tired of having her personal life be the topic of conversation, and dating Cole would be sure to spark up the chatter again. One of the drawbacks of small-town life…

Once the boys were dried and changed into their fuzzy pajamas, Maddy let them loose while she quickly tidied the bathroom. When she finally ventured into the living room, she found Cole sitting cross-legged on the floor, his lap piled with toys from the box. She stood in the doorway and just watched, smiling. Both her boys were running to the toy box and grabbing something and then showing it to Cole. He made the appropriate noises of approval, which just urged them on. Some of the toys they didn't even use anymore, like the rattles and plastic key ring. She laughed when Luke, always the excited one, reached in and nearly fell on his head trying to retrieve something. And when he ran to Cole, he tripped in his haste and landed on the carpet with a thump.

"Whoops," Cole said. "Easy, partner."

Luke's lower lip quivered and Cole got a look of panic on his face. Maddy was just about to step in when

Cole said, "Whatcha got there, Luke?" and it was just distraction enough to keep the tears at bay.

Plus he could tell Luke from Liam without much trouble. Not everyone could, but Cole paid attention.

"Having fun?" she asked softly, still standing with her shoulder resting on the doorway woodwork.

"Apparently I get to see the entire contents of that toy box."

She pushed herself away from the wall and went over to the play corner. "Congrats. They've hit bottom." She turned to Liam and Luke. "Boys, let's put everything back in the box!"

To demonstrate, she picked up a stuffed dog and carried it to the tub and dropped it in. Liam got the idea and took a plastic school bus, toddled over and flung it into the box. Not to be outdone by his brother, Luke grabbed something else and the game was on.

"They're pretty little to be doing so much, aren't they?" Cole asked. "Not that I have a lot of experience with kids."

Maddy laughed. "I think because there are two of them, and they have this competition going on. Luke can't stand for Liam to be one up on him. They were both walking at nine months. I was grateful and terrified all at once."

"I can see why."

She looked at him and noticed the food had dried on his shirt. "Would you like to change that, Cole? I think I still have one of Gavin's old sweatshirts around here somewhere."

He looked down. "I'm fine. It's just a little food."

"It's no trouble, really." She'd given most of Gavin's

things away, but she'd kept his law school hoodie. He'd loved it and she couldn't bear to part with it. No matter what he'd done.

She went to the bedroom and got it out of the closet. Considered for a moment. It was just a hoodie. She wasn't transferring any feelings for Gavin to Cole. She knew that with certainty as she held it in her hands, felt the thick, soft fabric in her fingers. Gavin was gone. Maybe she should just let go and move on. And lending a sweatshirt didn't have to have any deeper meaning than that.

Back in the living room, Cole's lap was nearly empty and Liam was standing rubbing his eyes. She handed Cole the shirt. "Here, you can borrow this. It's the least I can do considering you're wearing my son's supper."

Cole grinned. "Thanks."

"I'm going to get them each a bottle. They still like one at night before bed. I'll be back in a few minutes, okay?"

"Sure. We're just going to hang out here, right, guys?"

Luke went over to Cole, plopped down on his leg and started to babble.

He liked her sons. And her sons clearly liked him.

She filled the bottles and was heading back to collect the boys when she stopped dead in her tracks. Cole was changing out of his shirt, probably thinking she was in the kitchen and he had privacy. Maybe she should turn around and go back…but she didn't.

He stood in front of the sofa and unbuttoned the denim shirt, starting with the cuffs and then down the front. When he shrugged it off her mouth went dry.

She'd known he was lean, but he had muscles *everywhere*. It was winter and his skin had lost its summer tan, and his pecs had a sprinkling of dark chest hair. He reached for the hoodie and she watched, fascinated, as his shoulder muscles shifted and bunched with the simple movement. Arms went inside sleeves, his head poked through the top, and the shirt slid down over his flat belly.

Whew. There was no denying that she was attracted to him in the most elemental way possible. Sure, she'd found him nice and kind and good with her kids…but just now, as she'd watched him change, she'd responded like a woman.

It felt good. Really good.

Maddy cleared her throat and put on a bright smile as she stepped into the room as if nothing had happened. "Okay, who's ready for a bottle?" she asked.

Both boys ran to her and she laughed as she sat on the sofa, making room for each of them beside her. "Go get a book, Liam," she said, and Liam turned around and picked up one of their favorites from the pile, called *Bear Feels Scared*.

"Come on up, pumpkin," she said softly, hefting them up beside her and giving them each their bottle. "Okay. Ready?"

She was a little self-conscious as she read the story, knowing that Cole was listening, too, but this was part of their nighttime ritual, and she loved reading to her kids. As all of Bear's friends found him again, Liam crawled down off the sofa and got another book, a longer one called *Are You My Mother?* By the time she finished that one, eyelids were getting droopy and most of the milk was gone.

"I'm going to try to get them settled in bed," she murmured, looking over at Cole. He was sitting a few feet away, in the corner of the couch, his ankle crossed over his knee. The hoodie made him look cozy and comfortable and sexy in a weird, casual sort of way.

"Need help?" His voice was deep in the quiet of the room.

"I'm okay. I'll be back out in a few minutes. I hope." And he'd be waiting, wouldn't he? And they wouldn't have the twins between them, or be in a coffee shop, or have his brother sitting at the kitchen table.

They'd be alone.

She swallowed against the sudden nervousness that rushed through her.

She picked up Liam, who was fading faster than Luke, and then reached out for Luke, who helped by putting his hands up and around her neck.

They slept in separate cribs, and Maddy had a rocking chair situated in between them. Tonight, though, with the busy afternoon, short nap and fun evening, they both seemed tired and ready to be tucked in. She covered them with their blankets, tucked their favorite stuffed animals around them and made sure the nightlight was turned on. And then, when everything was quiet, she began to sing in a soft voice.

Luke stared up at her with wide eyes, as if absorbing every single syllable of the lullaby. Liam's lashes began to flutter straight away, and he rubbed his eye for a second before shoving his thumb in his mouth. Maddy knew from experience that once he was asleep, his lips would slacken and his thumb would pop out, forgotten.

When the song was done, she made sure she said, "Good night, sweeties," as she always did. Keeping to the routine seemed to help them settle.

And then, with her heart pounding madly, she left the bedroom, closed the door quietly behind her and returned to the living room.

The single corner lamp was burning, enveloping the room with a cozy glow. Cole was sitting in the same spot, his head leaned back against the cushion of the sofa, his ankle still crossed over his knee. "Get them to bed okay?" he asked quietly.

She nodded. "They were tired. It's been a busy day today, and tonight they had an audience for their antics." She smiled, stepped closer. "It's a big compliment, you know. Them wanting you to see all their toys. You're in the club."

He chuckled. "I can see why you're so crazy busy, though. My mom always said the two of us were four times the work of each of us individually."

"Sometimes," Maddy admitted. "And sometimes they have each other to keep themselves occupied and it gives me a break. I'm quite a bit younger than my brothers, John and Sam. They both left home when I was barely a teenager. We weren't that close, but I think Liam and Luke will be."

"And what about other kids? Do you want any?"

She sat down beside him, her pulse thundering in her ears. "That's...well, putting the cart before the horse. I haven't really thought about it much. That would mean I'd be remarried."

"Too soon, huh," Cole said.

"I like to ease into these things," she replied, and then laughed a little. "Cole, we have the strangest conversations. And I'm sorry I talk about the kids so much. It must get terribly boring."

"It's not." He moved his arm so it rested along the back of the sofa. "Believe me. The last girl I dated used to be a pageant queen. It probably sounds awful for me to say, because she was a nice girl for the most part. But when she launched into a good old pageant-days story, my eyes kind of glazed over."

Hmm. The last girl. She seemed to remember him being fairly serious about someone several years ago, though she couldn't quite remember the details. Now that she thought about it, she couldn't remember him being paired up with anyone since. Not for any amount of time. She wondered why.

He shifted lower in the corner of the sofa. "Come on over here and relax a little."

She was shy and nervous both as she wiggled closer to him on the sofa and tentatively leaned back against his shoulder. It was strong and warm and he left his arm along the sofa rather than dropping it down, keeping the embrace open. He was letting her take it slow, she realized, and she released a long breath.

"There," he said, a bit of humor touching his voice. "Nothing bad happened."

She laughed a little. "Sorry. I'm a bit nervous."

"Me, too. But it's just talking on the couch. Baby steps, remember?"

She nodded. He really did feel lovely and warm and cozy. She snuggled in a bit closer and this time his arm did come down from the top of the sofa and curled lightly around her. She closed her eyes. It had been so long since she'd been held. And with Cole it was only a little bit scary.

"Good?"

"Mmm-hmm." She closed her eyes. "Cole, why me? I mean, I've got baggage. A lot of it. And I'm prickly. I know it."

He chuckled and she felt the vibration of the sound through his chest and into her back. "Maybe I like a challenge. Besides, you're not the only one with baggage," he admitted. Before she could ask what he meant, he continued on. "Listen, what happened to you just made you cautious, that's all. You're not prickly. You're scared. I would be, too."

They let the thought sit for a few minutes, and then Cole spoke again. "I don't know, Maddy. I saw you that night at the library and I got thinking about how you're young and pretty and so damned strong and then…and then I couldn't stop thinking about you."

She turned a bit in his arms so that she could peer up into his face. "So the job offer? Was it because you were interested in dating me and that was your way in the door?"

He blushed. She saw the color infuse his cheeks, but his gaze held steady on hers. "That sounds so shallow. I just wanted to give you a helping hand because I like you. Christmas is such a rough time. Lots of people take on extra work over the holidays to help with expenses, you know."

And she'd considered just that, except she'd worried about babysitting. She nodded her acknowledgment and sat back in his arms again. "I know. And I appreciate it. To be honest, the last thing I was looking for was a date. But here we are. Maybe it just snuck up on both of us."

He shifted on the sofa, then turned her so she was facing him better. In the soft light she could make out the tiny scar just above his right eye, the way his irises seemed outlined with a black ring, the bow shape to his lips. She licked her own lips, which suddenly felt dry, and saw his gaze drop to where her tongue had wet the surface. Desire surged through her, terrifying by its very presence and exhilarating at the same time.

"It snuck up on me for sure," he admitted quietly. "You snuck up on me." And before she could think of anything to say, he dipped his head and touched his mouth to hers.

He was gentle, and took his time, and simply let himself linger for a while, teasing her lips with his until she felt herself start to relax a bit. She hadn't kissed anyone other than Gavin in…a lot of years. This felt different, strange and new, but exciting, too. As though she was transported back to a different time, when she was nineteen again or maybe twenty. There was a delicious flutter in her stomach and she tentatively lifted her hand and touched her fingers to the hair just above his ear.

That simple touch was all it took for Cole to shift his

weight a little, moving closer to her on the sofa, intensifying the kiss and taking it a bit deeper.

It blossomed into something beautiful.

Cole's arm slid around her ribs, his wide palm on the hollow of her back as he pulled her close. Maddy lifted her arms and twined them around his neck, opening her lips a little to let him in. There was desire between them but something more, too. She couldn't label it, but when Cole smiled against her lips, something in her heart rejoiced.

And when their mouths parted, he pulled her in close and just held her there in a hug. The backs of her eyes stung at the tenderness in his embrace.

"Was that okay?" he murmured softly.

She nearly said it was perfect, but truthfully she was a bit shaken by it all and didn't trust herself not to sound like an idiot, so she merely nodded.

"Want to try it again?"

She did, so much. So much, in fact, she thought it was probably a good idea if they didn't. "Baby steps," she whispered, resting her cheek on the curve of his shoulder. "I have a lot to think about."

He moved his head so it angled down to look at her. "Don't think too hard, okay? You're likely to talk yourself out of…well, whatever."

"You might be surprised." She lifted her chin. "I wasn't expecting this, Cole. I need some time to process. That's all."

"Sure." He ran a finger down her cheek. "Can't blame a guy for wanting more of a good thing."

And oh, wasn't that a lovely confidence boost?

"Can I tell you a secret?" she asked, feeling a little insecure but wanting him to understand.

"Of course."

"After Gavin died, and I heard the rumors, I...I wondered if maybe I was undesirable. If that's why he went to her."

His gaze softened. "Honey," he said, his voice smooth as silk, "you are one of the most desirable women I've ever met."

She laughed then. "You don't have to lay it on thick, Cole."

The soft look in his eyes hardened, and he sat back, taking her by the arms. "Look at me," he said firmly, and she obeyed. "Don't mistake me here. I know you want to move slow, and when you say slow down, I slow down. That has nothing—absolutely nothing—to do with what I want."

Her eyes widened and her chest cramped. He was so commanding right now, and she found it incredibly sexy. Cole was easygoing as far as she knew, but right now there was an intensity about him that was awesome.

"Maddy," he said, and his fingers tightened on her arms. "You're not ready, but that doesn't mean I don't want to kiss you again. To touch you." His eyes searched hers. "To carry you to your bed and make love to you."

"Cole," she murmured, awed and frightened at the same time. Not frightened of Cole, but of the fire that sparked to life between them as he said the words. Common sense was the only thing keeping her from throwing herself at him right now, peeling off that hoodie, feeling his skin on hers.

"You're desirable, Maddy, and don't you ever doubt it. And now I think I'd better go before we do get in over our heads."

But before he got up from the sofa, he put a hand along her cheek, rubbing his thumb on her cheekbone. And he smiled a little smile, one that went right to her heart. In that moment she realized that she couldn't have asked for a better person for her first romantic involvement after Gavin. And it wasn't just because he was sweet and sexy. Cole Hudson was kind and generous. He was a good man. And when Maddy was with him she felt safe.

She walked him to the door and got his coat off the peg as he pulled on his boots. "Thank you for supper," she said quietly, holding out the jacket so he could put his arms in.

"Thank you for the whole evening," he replied, shrugging it over his shoulders.

"Even the food on your shirt?" she joked, but he nodded.

"Especially the food on my shirt. Highlight of the night."

He was teasing again and she liked it, a lot. "Oh, really. I guess I know where I fit, then."

And then he surprised her. His arms came around her so fast she barely had time to react, and he planted a searing kiss on her mouth that made her weak in the knees and stole the breath from her lungs.

"That should clear up any confusion," he replied once he'd let her go.

Dazed, she stared up at him. "Okay, wow."

A grin spread across his face. "Thanks. There's more where that came from, just say the word."

"Get going, you nut."

He had his hand on the doorknob when she stepped forward. "Cole?"

"Yeah?" He turned back.

"Did you still want to, you know, help me get the tree inside tomorrow?"

His eyes glowed at her as he nodded. "If you'd like."

"Come around one thirty or so. That'll give me time to dig out the stand and stuff."

"Sounds good." He nodded again. "Good night, Maddy."

"Good night."

She watched him go down the walkway to his truck and climb inside. Once he was gone she closed the door and rested her back against it, trying to process everything that had happened today. She touched her fingers to her lips, feeling them tremble there just a bit. She'd had a date. A date! And the boys had been good and she'd been kissed and she was going to see him again...

Forget the tree outside. This was tantamount to a Christmas miracle!

Chapter Eight

It didn't take Cole long to figure out he was in big, big trouble.

He sat on the edge of his bed and put his head in his hands. Kissing Maddy had been a mistake. He'd foolishly made that comment on the wagon ride about wanting to spend time with her, testing the waters for her reaction. And he hadn't actually expected her to accept his offer of supper, low-key as it was.

He really hadn't prepared himself for how she'd looked when she came out of the bedroom after putting the boys to bed. Her sweater was soft and her hair a little bit mussed from dealing with the twins. He'd heard her singing in there, too, in the dark, and when she'd come out she'd had a contented, sleepy look about her. Cuddling on the couch had been the start, but her kisses… man, she kissed like an angel. All light and sweet and soft and with a pliancy that made a man want far more than he should expect.

She was so different from Roni. That fact had really hit home last night, leaving him temporarily defenseless. Roni's life had been dull and loveless, and he'd wanted to open her eyes to something more, to show her all the possibilities life had to offer. But Maddy's situation was different. She already knew love and kindness. She showed it every day in the tenderness and devotion to her kids, in the little things she did, the care she gave others. And that nurturing spirit was what drew him in and made him forget all his self-cautions about getting too close.

Now he was acting like a damned teenager, sitting on his bed and wondering what the hell to wear to her house to put up a Christmas tree.

Plaid shirt or sweater? Button-down dress shirt and jeans, perhaps? He got up and went to his closet, eliminating possibilities. He'd finally decided on the jeans and had tried on his third shirt when Tanner wandered into his room, his hair pushed to one side from sleep, dressed in sweats and a T-shirt.

"What's up, bruh?"

Cole gave him a sour look. "I've been up for hours. And did the chores. By myself."

Tanner ran his hand over his head. "Yeah, sorry. Late night." At Cole's wry smile, he added, "Not that. I was on call last night, and I ended up attending a couple of accidents thanks to black ice." He looked at Cole and frowned. "Where are you off to, anyway?"

"Out."

"Clearly. You've got on your good jeans and from the looks of your bed, you're trying to decide what to wear. What's the occasion?"

"Just, you know. Hanging out."

"So cryptic," Tanner replied, stepping inside the room. "So, what are you and Maddy up to today?"

"Who said I was seeing Maddy?" he asked, a little sharper than he meant to.

Tanner chuckled. "I've seen the way you look at her. And don't forget, I've been helping you pull off that secret Santa thing. So?"

Cole sat down on the bed, letting out a sigh. "I'm just helping her set up her tree."

"Right. And she issued this invitation when?"

Cole looked up at his younger brother. Cole was the older brother, but when it came to women he deferred to Tanner. His little bro never had a hard time getting the attention of the fairer sex. "Last night. We had some takeout at her place after the library thing."

"You dog."

"Careful, Tanner."

Tanner came in and picked a shirt off the bed, a deep red one with a fine plaid in navy and gold. "Wear this one. It's new and it's a good color without looking like you're trying too hard."

Cole took the shirt from his hands. "Am I an idiot? I mean, Maddy's great. But boy, is she gun-shy. Not that I can blame her. And she's got the kids... There's nothing simple about her, you know?"

Tanner put his hand on his brother's shoulder. "There's never anything simple about caring for a woman, Cole. If it's simple, it's not worth it."

"And you know this how?" Cole lifted an eyebrow. "From your three days of experience with marital bliss?"

"Ouch." Tanner took his hand away. "You want to know how I know? Because for me it's always been simple and it's never really been worth it. Not even with

Brittany. Which was why it only lasted three days, and that's all I'm going to say about that."

"Sorry. That was kind of a low blow."

Tanner shrugged. "No worries. I'm used to it."

Still, Cole felt guilty. No one liked having their past mistakes thrown up in their face all the time. "So you think Maddy's worth it?"

"I have no idea. Do you think she is?"

Cole thought about how she'd looked at him last night, as if he hung the moon and the stars. How she'd confessed that she'd worried about whether or not she was desirable, when his blood had been pounding through his veins all because of a simple kiss.

"She might be. She's different from any woman I've ever dated."

Tanner laughed again. "That's because she makes you work. Cole, you're a good-looking guy. And you're a nice guy. You've never had trouble getting female attention when you actually wanted it, and from what I can see you just sort of pick and choose, and date for a while, and then go your separate ways when you get bored. None of the women I can remember you dating was any sort of real challenge."

"Are you saying I'm only interested in Maddy because she's a challenge?"

Tanner shrugged again. "I don't know, are you?"

"You're sounding like a shrink." Cole slipped his arms into the shirt Tanner had picked. Darn, his brother was right. It was a good one. He started to do up the buttons.

"I don't mean to. She's just not the kind of woman

to mess with. She's been through enough and deserves better."

Cole stopped buttoning his shirt and looked closely at his brother. "Shit. Are you sweet on her, Tanner?"

Tanner shook his head. "No. But I'm not the insensitive jerk everyone seems to think I am, either."

"Aw, Tan…"

"Oh, for Pete's sake, I'm a grown man. And I haven't done a lot to change people's minds, have I?" He grinned. "All I'm saying is, think about why you're interested. And if you really, really care for her, I'm behind you one hundred percent."

Cole undid his jeans and went to work tucking in his shirt. "Mom warned me off her before they went on their trip. Said she had too much baggage."

"It's your life, not Mom's. Besides, she'd have instant grandkids."

"Don't even. The boys are cute, but I'm not sure I'm ready to be a dad. Hell, I'm just going over to put up a damned tree."

"Sure you are," Tanner said, and then with a whistle he left the bedroom, leaving Cole with a lot to think over. Including what his motives were. Because he knew that Tanner was wrong—it wasn't about getting bored and it wasn't about the challenge. The reason he never stuck it out was because he was scared of getting his heart handed back to him again.

One thing was becoming clear in his mind. There could be no more kissing. No more romance where Maddy was concerned. Because for the first time in a very long time, someone actually had the means to hurt him. He'd do better to keep his heart locked up where it belonged, wouldn't he?

Then he thought about kissing her and the soft sound she'd made when he'd pulled her close, and realized that sometimes things were far easier said than done.

MADDY WAS READY this time when Cole arrived. The boys were fed and cleaned up and dressed in adorable denim overalls and flannel shirts. The kitchen was tidied of lunchtime mess and Maddy had spun around the house this morning like something possessed, dusting and vacuuming and scrubbing the bathrooms. And yes, she'd used the playpen and the boys' favorite cartoons as babysitters, but she didn't do that very often and she wasn't going to feel guilty about it.

Right now they were on the floor playing with plastic farm animals. Maddy had made them a fenced-in area from the pieces of the set that clicked together. Liam put all the animals in the pasture, Luke threw them all out, they both giggled and then they started all over again.

It was exactly one thirty when Cole pulled up in her driveway. Maddy's pulse took a leap and she pressed her hand to her tummy. All morning she'd thought about last night's kiss and whether or not she was really ready to date someone. She wanted to—it had been so amazing to actually feel like a woman again instead of a frazzled mom. Desirable, rather than an object of pity.

And yet there was still a part of her that was unsure. She was smart enough to know it was all to do with her and her own insecurities. She'd been so wrong about Gavin; how could she possibly trust herself to get it right this time? She second-guessed everything. Even now, as Cole approached her front door, she wondered if she'd made a mistake inviting him today. If it was too much, or at least too soon… If he was really as awesome as he seemed, or simply too good to be true.

The doorbell rang and the boys froze, looked at Maddy and then scrambled to their feet. The arrival of company was always a cause of excitement.

Well, there was no backing out now. Maddy went to the door and opened it while the twins thumped about behind her. "Right on time," she said brightly. "Come on in."

Cole came in and removed his boots, then hung up his jacket, sticking his gloves in the pockets. "It's a bit warmer today," he commented.

The weather. Maddy didn't know if he was as nervous as she was, or if it was one of those forced to start a conversation things. "I heard we could get some more snow tonight." She led the way inside, on the way picking up Luke, who seemed intent on getting himself in the middle of things. "You're not busy with the festival today?"

Cole shook his head. "No. Today is an open skate at the park and snow golf. There's a carol sing tonight at the church. But I'm not required to be at any of them. Tomorrow, after everything's done and collected, we'll do the raffle draw from the shopping thing yesterday."

"It's ticked along like a good watch, then."

"So far, so good."

Luke strained from her arms and held his hands out to Cole. "Hey, buddy. You wanna come up?" He took him without missing a beat and settled him on his arm.

"Luke really likes you." There was something both

comforting and unsettling about seeing her baby so happy with Cole. "I never thought about it much, because they're so little. But maybe they really miss having a guy around."

Cole gave Luke a bounce, the expression on his face unreadable. "It's more likely that he recognizes me as the guy who got sprayed with food last night. It was a real bonding moment."

Liam pulled on her pant leg and she picked him up. "Do you want something to drink? I made a pot of coffee not long ago."

"Coffee sounds good," he replied, and they went to the kitchen.

She held Liam on her hip as she took out two mugs and spoons. "How do you take yours?" she asked, getting cream out of the fridge.

"One sugar, no cream," he replied.

She added his sugar, then just cream for herself, and suggested they go into the living room. Once there, she put Liam down on the floor. "Go play with your cows, sweet pea."

He scrambled down and Luke pushed out of Cole's arms to follow. Careful to not spill, Cole let him down and they ran back to their farm. Before long they were bouncing cows, horses and sheep through the pasture, making entertaining noises.

"Nice farm," Cole said, taking a seat at the end of the sofa and sipping his coffee.

"Thanks. It's one of their favorite toys. Sometimes they add dinosaurs to the mix." She grinned. "I was thinking we'd wait until nap time and then bring the tree in. Probably easier when they're not underfoot."

"You're probably right."

"I found the stand and decorations this morning, though." She sat back against the cushions. "I'm looking forward to the boys seeing it, actually. Last year they were too little."

A chicken went flying and dinged Luke in the head, and he started to wail. "Liam, gentle. Luke, come here, Mommy will kiss it." Luke toddled over, Maddy kissed his forehead and the crying ceased immediately.

"Wow, like magic," Cole said drily.

"Wouldn't it be nice if a kiss could always fix up hurts?" Maddy sighed. "It's a lot simpler when you're a kid, that's for sure."

"Isn't that the truth."

Maddy felt the need to change the subject, so she took another sip of her coffee and asked, "How's your parents' trip going?"

They chatted for the next twenty minutes about their families and the festival and basic small talk. When it was nearly two, Luke came over with a board book and crawled up on her knee. "Buh," he said, holding it out.

"You want me to read you a book?"

"Buh," he repeated.

She looked over at Cole. "Yesterday was busy and they've been up since seven thirty. It's just about nap time."

She started reading the little book and when she got to the end and gave it back to him, he handed it to her again.

So she read it a second time. This time Liam came over and climbed up on the sofa beside them. Both boys were mellowing out substantially, and when Luke asked her to read it a third time, she laughed and obliged. By that point, Liam had leaned back against Cole and his eyelids were drooping. Luke's were nearly closed, his head doing an unstable bobble now and again.

"Come on, bubba. Let's put you to bed." She cradled him in her arms and walked softly to their room, where she gently put him down and covered him up. "Have a good sleep, Luke."

He stared at her for a moment. One thing she did appreciate about the boys was they'd learned to be patient right from the start, that sometimes they'd have to wait or soothe themselves. There wasn't a peep out of him as she went back to get Liam.

His eyes were wide-awake now, though he still leaned against Cole's strong body. Maddy reached for him and he came willingly, curling his hands around her and tucking his face against her neck. She rocked back and forth for a few minutes, crooning softly. Cole smiled up at her. "He's out."

"They've been so busy lately, they've been sleeping really well. And when they're busy, I'm exhausted," she joked. She swayed back and forth a few more times. "I'll be right back, I hope."

She tucked Liam in and made sure the thermostat was set to a comfortable temperature, and then shut the door and went to join Cole.

"There. They should be good for ninety minutes or so. Should we get this set up?"

"By all means." Cole put his mug down on the table. "Where do you want to put it?"

"Right in front of the window." She smiled. "I generally just move that chair a bit to the right and move that speaker, and it sits right in the middle."

"Well, let's do that first and then bring it in."

It took no time at all to adjust the furniture, and then Maddy retrieved the tree stand and skirt while Cole went out to the doorstep and brought in the bushy tree. Needles dropped as he moved it across the floor, and more still as she got on her hands and knees to hold the stand and help him guide the trunk into the hole. As he held it steady, she tightened the wing nuts until they were tight and the tree was straight. "How's that look?" she asked.

"Good. Tanner..." He stopped talking abruptly, and she sat back on her knees and looked up at him.

"Tanner what?"

"Tanner will be jealous," he said, brushing his hands together. "It's a great tree. Nice and full all the way around."

"Hand me that tree skirt, will you?"

Cole handed her the wedge-shaped folded fabric and she spread it out. She loved this skirt. It had a creamy gold satin background, with appliquéd holly and berries and stars all over it, bordered by a rich red fringe. She smoothed it out, tied the ribbons at the back to hold it in place around the stand, and slid out from beneath the tree.

"Wow. That didn't take any time at all," she said, hopping to her feet. "Thank you so much. It would have been a real circus trying to get that in the stand by myself. And I do still love a real tree, even though the new artificial ones are so practical."

"Me, too. Dad suggested one of those pre-lit ones a few years ago and Mom had a fit. We've always had a real tree." He smiled at her. "Dad has a chipper. We just chip it up and send it back to nature."

Maddy admired the tree, imagining how good it was going to look with the decorations on. "Know what one of Mom and Dad's neighbors do? They have a tree-burning party. They set up a bonfire pit in their backyard and invite everyone to bring their trees over, and they have drinks and food and light it up. It's really fun."

Cole reached for his coffee, which had to be lukewarm at best right now. "Is that what you're doing for Christmas? Spending it with your family?"

Maddy sighed. "Probably. I've been meaning to ask my parents if they want to come over Christmas morning and watch the boys open their presents. Dinner's at their house, so we can have breakfast here." To be honest, the thought of Christmas morning was both exciting and, well, depressing. Maddy loved the holiday, but she had a hard time rustling up a lot of Christmas spirit. It was all about making it good for the boys. But the holiday was pretty lonely on her own.

Now the task of decorating the tree was before her and she blinked. Last year it had been a real production, with the four of them in the living room, carols playing, the perfect little family. As she stared at the green branches, her vision blurred. It was time she faced a truth she'd been putting off. The past and her rosy memories of it had been a lie, and she needed to accept it and, more importantly, move past it. The anger and bitterness were eating her up inside. That wasn't good for her, or the boys, and she had to start getting on with her life.

Maybe Christmas was the perfect time to do that.

"Hey, are you okay?"

Cole's soft voice interrupted her thoughts. She quickly swiped a finger beneath her lashes. "Actually, yes. I think I am." She turned to him and smiled, feeling lighter than she had in months. "I've had such a hard time letting go. Holding on to the past, you know? And then getting angry about it. I'm tired of being angry, Cole. I think it's time I start over."

"That sounds very healthy," Cole replied, but he didn't smile. His expression was completely sober. He could have no idea how much she appreciated him taking her seriously and not giving her a patronizing smile or some platitude.

She blinked away the remaining moisture in her eyes. "You know, I think I'm just so hurt that nothing is going to be the way we planned, and I dealt with it by being mad and passing blame. But it doesn't make sense to live my life mad at someone who isn't even here, does it?"

Cole shook his head. "Not really." He sighed. "You know, I think we're more alike than either of us realized."

"We are?" She was puzzled. Cole never seemed mad or angsty or any of the things she'd felt over the last months. He was always so *together*.

"I was in love once." He gave a dry chuckle. "It seemed like everything was great, and then she was just...gone. I'd like to say I'm over it, but I'm more gun-shy than I care to admit."

"Roni, right? I seem to remember you being in a relationship for a couple of years."

He nodded. "Yeah."

He didn't say more. She supposed it was a big thing that he'd even said anything about it.

"Did you think she was the one?"

Maddy held her breath after she asked the question. They were getting really personal here. But it was good, too. She'd felt so alone in her misery and Cole had seemed too perfect. No flaws, no vices. Knowing he understood from experience made him seem a little more...normal.

"Yeah," he said softly. "I did."

"What happened?"

He didn't answer for so long that she thought perhaps he wasn't going to. But finally he let out a big sigh and met her gaze. "I gave her everything I had. But it wasn't enough. Or at least, it wasn't what she wanted. So she left. It's been pretty hard for me to open up to anyone since."

Maddy's heart ached for him. She knew exactly how that felt, and it was so, so lowering to a person's self-esteem. "I'm really sorry, Cole."

He tried to smile. "Hey, it was a long time ago. Don't sweat it."

She smiled back. He passed it off as being nothing, but she knew it wasn't. "Don't kid a kidder. It's no fun when someone hands your heart back to you with a *no, thanks*."

"True enough. Anyway, I thought maybe you should know. I really do understand when you talk about moving slow." He reached over and squeezed her fingers, and then let her hand go.

A new strength started to build within her, and it felt good. It felt as if she was starting to be in control of her own life again rather than lamenting the current state of affairs, looking forward to the future rather than being mired in the past. "Cole, neither of us can change what's happened. But there's one thing we can control, and that's what we do right now, in this moment. And you know what? Today I choose simple holiday joy and goodwill. How about you?"

Cole chuckled, the mood lightening. "Joy and goodwill, huh? That sounds easy enough. I'm in. What's first on the agenda?"

She looked up at him. Lordy, he was so handsome. Neither of them was ready for anything serious. Their conversation had just proved that. And yet there was no denying that they liked each other, so she treated him to a huge grin. "Decorations. And we only have about an hour, so roll up your sleeves, bucko. It's time Christmas got real around here."

They left the heavy topic of broken hearts behind; Cole actually did as she asked and started rolling up his sleeves. She dashed to the basement for the first box of decorations and came upstairs again, depositing it on the sofa. "Come on, there are three more. Time to use those muscles."

Together they brought up the decorations, and then Maddy started going through them, seeing what was what. "Lights," she announced, pulling out a bag. "Lights go on first. Let's test them."

She was on a roll now. Cole started stringing the multicolored lights on the tree as she plugged in each set and made sure they worked, replacing bulbs when necessary. It was the longest part of the process, but once he had all the lights at his feet, she dug through the box and got out other decorations. A pretty wreath for above the fireplace, some holiday knickknacks for the mantel. Cute candy-cane place mats for the kitchen table, handcrafted Advent calendars for the twins that Maddy and Gavin had bought last year with the intent to use them this Christmas. Plus plastic dishes—little trays and bowls and a mug and plate set for Santa's milk and cookies, as well as Frosty and Rudolph plates and cereal bowls for the boys.

She bustled around, putting everything out, thinking how she wouldn't have to worry about putting things up high as the years went on.

"The lights are done," Cole announced, getting up from his knees, where he'd been putting the last ones around the bottom. "What do you think?"

"They look great!" Maddy saw he'd taken care to keep the spaces even so there weren't any blank spots. "Okay. Now the garland." She reached into the box and took out ropes of the red metallic stuff. "I'll do this part if you'll check in the box for the star that goes on the top? You're taller than me, anyway."

He dug around in the box while she looped the garland in festive swoops, working her way all around the tree. She ran out one row short of the bottom, but merely shrugged. This tree was a little fuller than last year's, and the stuff on the bottom would only attract little fingers, anyway. Beside her, Cole reached up and put the star on the top and plugged it into the first set of lights.

"It's getting there."

"It is." She grinned at him. "Know what? We need some Christmas music." She dashed off to the bedroom for the little portable stereo she kept in there, brought it out and plugged it in and then went to the CD cabinet in the corner to pluck out some of the old Christmas CDs.

"There's holiday music on its own channel, you know," Cole said. "You could just turn on the TV."

She would not be embarrassed; Cole already knew her financial situation was tight. "I canceled most of our cable a few months ago," she admitted. "We just get the basic channels now."

Cole was the one who blushed. "Oh."

She shrugged. "I didn't really need it, anyway. I've got my phone, too, but the stereo doesn't have Bluetooth, so that's out. But it doesn't matter." She was determined that nothing was going to dampen her enjoyment today. "The oldies are the best versions, anyway. This CD will be perfect."

She hit play and then reached for the first box of ornaments as Bing Crosby's smooth voice quietly sang "White Christmas." The sunny day turned cloudy in anticipation of the coming snow, and the lights from the tree created a cozy glow as they hung ornaments on the tree. Bit by bit it came together until they stood back and viewed the finished product. Maddy got a lump in her throat. It was beautiful. And it was hers. And she was going to get a jump on New Year's resolutions and make one right now: from now on she was going to live in the present, and do it on her own two feet.

"Hang on," she said, and dashed to the kitchen. Moments later she joined him again and handed him a glass. "Eggnog," she said, grinning. "I splurged at the grocery store."

"It only comes once a year," he agreed. "The tree looks great, Maddy."

"It does. When we were standing here looking at it, I made a resolution that I'm going to start living in the present. So…" She held up her glass. "To new beginnings."

They clinked glasses and his gaze held hers while the delicious feeling of anticipation began to spread over her again. When she'd said "New beginnings," she hadn't exactly meant new relationships, but he was standing here before her, looking all hunky and gorgeous, and they'd decorated the tree together and Nat King Cole was crooning on the stereo…

"You forgot something," he said softly, and after taking a drink of his eggnog he put the glass down and reached into the last box.

When he straightened, he was holding a sprig of plastic mistletoe in his hand.

"Oh," she said, and her voice sounded just a bit breathless.

He took the glass from her hand, put it beside his on the side table and returned to stand in front of her. Right in front of her. So close that if she lifted her hands they'd be pressed against the front of his shirt and his broad chest…

She looked down. Her hands *were* pressed against his chest, the warmth of it against her skin as his breathing quickened. He held the mistletoe up over their heads. "Be a shame to break a tradition," he murmured, his eyes dark and mesmerizing.

"A shame," she echoed.

He took his time, and when his lips finally touched hers she could barely breathe. It was as good as last night...no, better. There was anticipation and nerves but not the first-time nerves that had made her so jumpy. There was a sweetness and purity to it that reached in and wrapped around her heart. It was a perfect Christmas kiss, under the mistletoe, in front of a Christmas tree, with the taste of eggnog still on their lips and a soft carol on the air.

Their lips parted and she let out a blissful sigh. "Cole," she whispered. "What are we starting here?"

He didn't answer, but he dropped the mistletoe on the floor and pulled her into his arms for a deeper, more satisfying kiss. Her head was swimming with it all. The feel of his strong arms wrapped around her, the scent of his cologne on his clothes, the way his teeth nipped gently at her lower lip, causing a dart of desire straight to her core.

A cry echoed down the stairs, muffled by the distance and the bedroom door, but definitely an impatient howl.

It was the worst—and best—time for the boys to wake up from their nap.

Chapter Nine

Maddy pulled away, her eyes still dazed and her body humming. Cole, too, had a look of surprise about him, as if this was more than he'd expected, somehow. As if reality had smacked him in the face like a splash of ice-cold water. Maddy wasn't sure which boy was crying, but they were really tuning up now. Had they been awake for a while already and she hadn't heard their fussing?

"I have to go," she whispered, stepping back. "Get the boys."

"And show them the tree." The words were innocuous enough, but there was a strain in Cole's voice that hadn't been there before.

Right. Big mistake and he was regretting it, wasn't he?

She rushed off to the bedroom, her emotions in turmoil as she opened the door and saw both Luke and Liam standing up in their cribs having a shouting contest. "All right, you two, I'm here," she said, stepping inside.

The noise changed from shouting to delighted squeals and bouncing on the mattresses. "Let's get you changed first," she said, picking up Liam. In no time flat she had him in a fresh diaper, deposited him in Luke's crib, picked up Luke and repeated the process. All the while she was thinking about Cole.

Their kisses today had been amazing. Phenomenal. Unburdened, she realized. It seemed that a weight had lifted, allowing a new intimacy. Could it be that a change of attitude had accomplished all that? But then... when the boys had started crying, Cole had looked almost upset. Lordy, she'd been out of the dating scene for so long that she had no idea how to read the clues.

With both babies in her arms, she took a deep breath. "You ready, boys? Mama has something to show you." She started out of their room and down the stairs. "We've got a Christmas tree. Look, isn't it pretty?"

She turned the corner and there was Cole, standing in front of the tree, his eggnog in his hand again. Her pulse picked up at the sight of him. But then she looked at her sons and her heart simply melted.

Eyes as big as saucers, they stared at the tree. Two little mouths formed perfect O's, and the lights were reflected in their huge blue eyes.

"Do you like it?" Maddy put them down. "Don't touch, now. Just look. Pretty."

Liam approached it carefully, stared up to the top, then back to the bottom and a particularly shiny ornament. "Buh," he said. It was his favorite almost word. As far as Maddy was concerned, it showed his approval.

Luke took a few steps forward, then raced back to Maddy. "Up," he said, holding out his hands. She lifted him up and took him over to the tree, where he pointed at individual ornaments and made unintelligible but what sounded like approving noises.

She looked over at Cole.

"You are so good with them," Cole said. "So patient."

She laughed and put Luke down again. "Not always. Believe me. I just try to hold it in until I'm alone."

"You put them first. And they know it, because even at their age they're happy and secure."

"They'll always come first," she vowed, lifting her chin a little to look up at him.

"Maddy, you asked what we were starting. The truth is, I don't know." His gaze searched hers. "Maybe your idea of living in the present is a good one. Just take it day by day."

Maddy considered. She wondered if seeing Cole was a mistake. There was a big possibility that neither of them was emotionally ready for romance. But then, day by day was a pretty small commitment when all was said and done.

"Day by day sounds nice," she answered. She broke eye contact briefly to make sure the boys weren't getting into trouble, then looked up at him again.

"So how about I take you to dinner sometime next week? I'll pay for a sitter. We can have an evening out, just the two of us."

Maddy bit down on her lip. "To dinner?" The idea of an actual date, a public one, gave her a lot of misgivings. Kisses in private were one thing. But going out, particularly in a place like Gibson, made a statement. When you did that, you were a *couple*.

"You know, where people order food and it's brought to them and they eat it?"

She couldn't help but smile a little. "Yes, I know. I'm just… Well, I'm not sure that's a good idea."

When Cole didn't say anything, she elaborated. "It's just that for the past six months, I've felt like people were whispering behind my back all the time. And not always bad stuff, but my life became news. I don't want this to be news, Cole. At least not yet, until we're sure. Or ready. Or…heck, I don't know. I think I'd be on edge, though, and not much fun to be around."

"We've been out together before. Yesterday, on the wagon ride. Coffee at the Grind. The only difference is how we categorize it. Heck, we don't even have to call it a date. It could be sharing a meal or hanging out." He smiled and she thought again how he could be so darned charming.

He was right in a way, too. Maybe the perception was all in her head. But then, maybe they'd already provided fodder for gossip. "People might already be talking," she said plainly. "I just want to keep things more private. At least for now. Can we do that?"

Disappointment marked his face and she felt bad about it. "Cole, you didn't do anything wrong. I love that you asked me. I'd just rather stay out of the public eye for a while."

He nodded, but she could tell there were things he wasn't saying. It was in the way his jaw was set and his lips were pursed.

She put a hand on his arm. "I'm sorry. I know this must seem exactly the opposite of what I said earlier about letting go of the past. I've been the topic of conversation and speculation enough, and I just want some privacy. That's all."

"What if I come up with a compromise?"

She hesitated. "If I say yes that means I'm committed. Sneaky." She smiled a little. "How about I say maybe? It'll depend on what it is."

"I'll let you know. Now, I should probably be going. Tanner's going to go crazy if I leave him to do the chores on his own tonight. Even though I did them by myself this morning." He grinned. "You'll be by the house tomorrow, though?"

"You still want me there?"

"Of course, why wouldn't I?" His brows pulled together in the middle.

Maddy could have bitten her tongue. She'd assumed that it had been a pity position, a made-up way to give her some help. But he looked sincerely perplexed. Maybe the offer had been genuine all along.

"Oh, never mind. I'll get there around nine. I work at one instead of two, though, so I'll have to leave by twelve fifteen to get the boys to day care and then on to work."

"Sounds perfect to me."

They looked around at the boys. Luke had found Maddy's eggnog glass and had taken sips from it, leaving a streak of creamy white down the front of his shirt and the glass as well, which was forming a ring on the table. Liam was sitting on the floor, playing with a plush ornament he'd plucked from the tree.

Maddy sighed. "See what happens when I get distracted? And this is why the soft ornaments are at the bottom of the tree. I see it's going to be an interesting few weeks."

"But fun, I hope. With lots of that Christmas spirit you've been looking for."

His eyes held a twinkle. It seemed the earlier awkwardness was forgiven, or at least forgotten for the time being. She liked that about Cole. He was easygoing, and that was something she particularly needed right now.

"It's getting there," she admitted. "Today helped."

"Then I think you should help us decorate our tree when the time comes. Mom and Dad are home in nine more days and it'd be nice to have the house decorated for when they return."

"Now that I can do." She grinned up at him, then reached down and took the ornament from Liam and hung it back on the tree. "Don't touch, Liam."

She walked Cole to the door, waited as he put on his coat and boots. "Thanks for coming over. For the help and for the company. It would have sucked decorating the tree alone."

"I'm glad I could help."

She reached out and took his hand. "You have. More than you know. Thanks for being understanding."

Cole leaned down and kissed her lightly. "I'll see you in the morning," he murmured, then reached for the door handle. At the last minute he looked up and at the boys. "'Bye, Luke and Liam."

Maddy's heart gave a stutter as both of them stopped what they were doing and looked at Cole. And then

Liam, bless him, grinned a toothy smile and flapped his hand in goodbye.

"In the morning," she parroted, and held the door as he went outside into the cold afternoon.

COLE HUDDLED AGAINST the bitter wind as he guided his horse out of the pasture and toward home again. Tanner rode behind him, neither of them saying anything in the frosty morning. After morning chores they'd gone out on horseback to move part of the herd to a different pasture with new stacks. Normally it was fun, but the wind chill had bitten at his face and his fingers were cold inside his gloves. He was glad that job was over and he could do something else for the afternoon. Something inside where it was warm.

"Hey, hold up," Tanner called, and Cole reined in a little, allowing Tanner to catch up to him.

"A cup of coffee is sure gonna be good," Tanner said, hunching his shoulders. "It's a cold one today." The white cloud of his breath seemed to hang in the air as he spoke.

The mention of coffee reminded Cole that Maddy was going to be at the house when they went in. God, he was so mixed up about that. Not even twenty-four hours ago he'd resolved that nothing could happen. He'd been certain they would be just friends—and then he ended up kissing her under the mistletoe and asking her to dinner.

Was it the challenge? Maybe Tanner was right and Cole was wrong. He looked over at his brother and took a deep breath. They didn't usually talk about this sort of thing. But he found he needed a sounding board, and Tanner, for all his faults, was not one to judge.

"Hey, Tanner? What you said yesterday, about me getting bored with women... Do you think I'm interested in Maddy just because she's, well, she's hard work?"

"So she hasn't fallen into your arms at the snap of your fingers?"

Cole wondered if it was possible to blush when he was this cold. "Be serious."

"I am serious. This is about Roni, isn't it? You never got over her leaving you."

The words stung. "That was a long time ago, Tanner. Granted, I'm not in a hurry to give someone the ammunition to hurt me, but there's nothing wrong with being cautious."

Tanner started laughing. "Cole, this is the first time I've seen you tying yourself in knots over a woman in years."

"Glad you think it's funny." He wiggled his fingers inside his gloves, relieved when the barn came into view.

"I think it's awesome. What's funny is that you don't get it."

"Don't get what?"

"Why it's so hard for you. Cole, I don't know if you've noticed, but you have a bit of a rescue complex."

Cole frowned and looked over at Tanner. His brother seemed serious now, no laughing at all. "What on earth are you talking about?"

Tanner sighed. "I know you loved Roni, but what you really loved was being her knight in shining armor. Or leather, as the case may be." He smiled briefly at his own joke. "Roni's life growing up was rough. We all know that. You swept in and tried to take care of her and make everything better. And for a while it worked and you guys were happy. But it wasn't enough to base forever on, you know?"

"What was I supposed to do, then? Not help?" Hell, Tanner knew little about it. Roni's mom had been abused by her husband before they split up. They'd had hardly any money, and Roni hated being at home. She used to say that it smelled like stale cigarettes and disappointment.

"Of course not. But it's not your job to fix things for everyone, either. You can't take all that on yourself. After a while it…"

He hesitated.

"It what?"

The air was clear, so for a few moments the only sound on the wind was the steady but muffled clopping sound of hooves on hard-packed snow and dirt. "You mean well. But it can make the person on the receiving end feel like a burden. Or…well, incapable. Like you don't trust them to fix things for themselves."

That was a little too insightful for it to be out of the blue or off-the-cuff. "Do I do that to you, Tan?"

Tanner shrugged. "Maybe a little. I know you're the responsible one and I'm the goof-off, but I can handle more than you think."

Cole didn't know what to say. Tanner was younger than he was. He'd always felt protective and responsible for him, but maybe he'd been too protective. Looking back, he realized Tanner had tried a lot of unexpected things. Like his brief marriage, and doing his EMT training. "I've held you back, haven't I?" He felt like a heel even asking.

"Hell, Cole, you're my big brother. You just… Well, you cast a long shadow sometimes. It makes it hard to live up to, so I acted out a bit from time to time." Tanner's sideways grin was back, though, and Cole felt relief slide through him. His brother didn't harbor hard feelings, at least.

"Anyway," Tanner finished, "hopefully I've grown up enough to figure out it's not a competition."

"I never realized," Cole said, shifting in his saddle. The leather creaked in the cold.

"Of course you didn't. The thing is, Roni was young and at a disadvantage, and you were a little older and had your shit together. At first I bet it was really great. But in the end it was probably too much, you know? I know the breakup hurt you. You felt like you gave her everything and she threw it back in your face."

That was it exactly.

"The problem is," Tanner informed him, "that you're doing the same thing with Maddy. Riding to her rescue. But you're also guarding your heart and it's creating this tug-of-war that's driving you crazy."

Cole tugged on the reins and halted the horse. "Shit."

Tanner stopped, too. "What?"

Cole let out a sigh, a cloud of breath puffing in the air before his face. "Do I really do that? Try to fix everything?"

Tanner rested his reining hand on the saddle horn

and lifted his other hand, raising his fingers as he item-
ized the list.

"You offered her the job at the house, even though
we could have managed just fine until Mom and Dad
got home. You put new tires on her car. You bought
her a Christmas tree. You bought her dinner and then
went back to help her decorate the tree. I'm running out
of fingers here, Cole, and it's only been a few weeks."

"Am I wrong to want to help?" He suspected his
brother had hit the nail on the head, too. Every time he
found himself getting close to Maddy, he backed off in
a hurry. Only to discover he couldn't seem to stay away.

Tanner nudged his mount, starting along the lane
again. "Are you wrong? No, of course not. You're a good,
generous, upstanding guy. I like Maddy, and I told you
that. But you might want to sort out *why* you're doing it.
Is it because you need to be needed? Or do you really,
honestly care about her?"

They were quiet for a while as they rode back to the
ranch yard. They were nearly to the barn when Cole
spoke up. "Hey, Tanner? How'd you get so smart about
that stuff?"

Tanner looked back at him, but the expression on
his face was tight and grim. "We're cut from the same
cloth, or didn't you realize that? You're not the only
one in the family to mistake how someone feels. For
me it was Britt. For you it was Roni. It makes a man a
little gun-shy."

Cole thought about Tanner's most public mistake—
his brief Vegas marriage a few years back. Now he vol-
unteered as an EMT and helped people that way. Cole

had always thought it was rather noble of his brother, but now he wondered if it was something else. A form of rebellion, perhaps, or Tanner's way to help people while keeping himself detached from them on a personal level.

Either way, Tanner had given him lots to think about.

They were at the barn now and they halted, each dismounting quietly and gathering reins in their hands to lead the horses inside. "Hey, thanks for being a sounding board this morning," Cole said as he tied the gelding and reached for the cinch strap.

"That's what brothers are for," Tanner answered, and clapped a hand on Cole's shoulder in solidarity before moving away. "But that's enough of the touchy-feely crap for one day. When's the farrier due out again?"

The subject was changed and the focus returned to ranch operations—at least for the time being. When lunchtime arrived, the strange, weightless feeling returned to Cole's stomach, simply from knowing that Maddy was waiting inside.

And he still had no idea what he was going to do about it.

Chapter Ten

The morning at Cole's was the most difficult Maddy had had yet.

Luke appeared to be teething, and his slight fever and whiny temperament grated on Maddy's nerves. She tried cooling teething rings and numbing gel, which only created more drool until she simply left a bib around his neck all the time to keep his clothing dry. Baby acetaminophen helped after a while, and he crashed on the floor on the blanket, but by then Liam was bored of being by himself and begged for attention. Trying to get the sheets washed and the beds made up was nearly impossible, and she burned the first pan of cookies she baked and needed to open a window to let out the smoky stench. By noon she was ready to pull her hair out, but at least she'd managed the bedding and baked the rest of the cookies without incident, and there was a batch of spaghetti sauce on the stove so Cole and Tanner just had to make pasta for dinner.

And then she realized she hadn't made lunch. For anyone. And she had to get the boys to day care and be at work by one.

When Cole came in, she was frantically flipping grilled cheese sandwiches on a griddle and stirring tomato soup on the stove. "I'm so sorry," she said, pushing the hair off her face that had come out of her ponytail. "Luke is teething and Liam's clingy and I lost track of time…"

"Relax," he said, walking into the kitchen and taking the spatula from her hands. "Tanner's making a quick run into the hardware store, so it's just me. And you've got four sandwiches on the go." He checked his watch. "Besides, weren't you supposed to be out of here soon?"

She checked her watch. Twelve twenty. "Dammit," she muttered, reaching for a plate. "I'm sorry, Cole. I should have had this done and cleaned up for you."

"Maddy. It's fine. Have you and the boys eaten?"

She shook her head as she rushed around, slamming things back into cupboards.

"Here." He shoved a sandwich into her hand. "Take two minutes and eat a sandwich. I can't eat four. What do the boys need?"

"I can leave their lunch at the day care. I don't like to, but I can."

She looked at the sandwich. She shouldn't, but it was a heck of a long time until dinner. She sighed, took a bite. Grilled cheese was perhaps the best comfort food on the planet. Something about crispy bread and butter and melted cheese just soothed.

"See?" Cole took a bite and chewed about a quarter of one sandwich. "Food. Breathing. Necessities of life."

She swallowed. "Everything just seemed to work against me today."

He smiled. "Well, some days are like that. I can wash up from this. And there are cookies. And something in that pot over there. It's all good."

She was chewing again. "Spaghetti sauce," she said around her mouthful of sandwich. "And I stripped the beds and washed the sheets."

"Perfect. Finish that and I'll dress the boys."

She wanted to protest, but he had already grabbed the blue and red suits and proceeded to put Liam's on Luke. It didn't matter. She shoved the rest of the sandwich into her mouth, wiped her hands and went to help.

There was no time for anything remotely romantic or intimate or…anything. Maddy wasn't sure if she was disappointed or relieved. She still had so many mixed feelings where Cole was concerned. Mostly that she liked him, probably too much, and felt as though she shouldn't. And today he was acting as if nothing had ever happened between them. He was just being friendly and helpful and that was it.

"There. All ready. Do you want some help getting them to the car?"

"That'd be great, Cole. I really am sorry."

"Will you stop apologizing?" He shrugged into his coat and pulled on a pair of winter boots but left them untied. "Oh. And I forgot to pay you for last week." He reached into his pocket and pulled out some bills. "Here. Three days, right?"

She hesitated, and he held out his hand. "Maddy, come on. You're not cooking and cleaning in my house and not getting paid for it." He shook the bills.

When he put it like that, she couldn't argue. It just felt

strange and wrong, considering how they'd been kissing lately. Reluctantly she took the money and tucked it in her pocket. She swallowed against a tightness in her throat. It was almost as though those intimate moments between them had never happened at all.

"Okay, slugger. Here we go." Cole picked up Luke, shouldered the diaper bag and left Liam for Maddy. At the car he helped fasten them in and opened her door.

It all happened so fast that she barely had time to breathe. At this rate she was going to get to work spooled up like a top.

"Hey," he said, standing in front of her door so she couldn't get in. "Drive safely. Don't speed, okay? Tanner's been to too many accidents lately."

"I will."

"Nothing is so important that a few extra minutes will matter, you know?"

Some of the tension left her body. "I know. This morning just got me all discombobulated."

"Okay. Oh, and you forgot something else, too."

"I did?" She ran her list through her mind. Yes, she'd hoped to do a bit more cleaning today, but what had she forgotten?

He leaned forward and cupped his hand around her neck. "One of these," he said, and touched his lips to hers.

It only took a few seconds of delicious contact for her to melt against him. The tension in her muscles eased as he took his time, giving her a thorough goodbye kiss that would leave her body humming for a good long time.

Their lips parted and she took a nice, slow breath. "That was nice."

"I know. You better now?"

She looked up into his eyes, feeling slightly dazed but much calmer. "Yes, thank you."

He smiled. "Then get going. I'll call you later."

"Okay."

"Okay."

She got in the car and he shut the door behind her, then headed back to the house, his untied boots scuffing in the snow. She refused to worry about the time as she drove away. Five or ten minutes wasn't going to get her fired, and she went in early or stayed late often enough that it bought her some leeway. She dropped off the boys at Sunshine Smiles, leaving instructions to give Luke another dose of medicine if he needed it and their containers of lunch that they'd missed. Then on to the library, where she quickly stowed her coat and bag and joined Eloise in the day's work.

"You look frazzled," Eloise noted. "Everything okay?"

"Yeah." Maddy smiled. "Crazy morning. And Luke's teething." She didn't mention anything about Cole. No one knew she was working for him and she'd like to keep it that way.

"That'll try anyone's patience," Eloise replied with a sympathetic smile. "Why don't you take a few minutes, grab a tea from the lunchroom?" Her gaze darted to Maddy's hair. "Redo your ponytail."

"Oh, am I a mess? Darn it…"

"Like I said, just a little frazzled. I'll man the desk for a few minutes. Go get some mint tea."

"Thanks, El."

The beverage and few moments in the staff bathroom

were just what she needed. She came back to the front feeling slightly refreshed and much more relaxed. The mint tea was soothing and she went to work at the circulation desk with a renewed energy.

At three-thirty there was an influx of people; school let out for the day and several students came in with textbooks in hand to find tables for study groups. A few parents came with kids to pick out new books, and several returns were dropped in the drop box. Maddy was in the process of issuing a new library card to a very excited first grader when a deliveryman came through the doors holding a big basket.

She looked up. "Hi, can I help you?"

"Are you Maddy Wallace?"

"That's me." She looked at the basket in his arms. It was wrapped in clear cellophane with tiny snowflakes on it and tied with a sparkly silver ribbon.

"Delivery for you. Can you sign for it, please?"

"Excuse me just a moment," she said to the mom and daughter. She took a pen and signed the delivery slip. "You're sure this is for me?"

"Positive. Says Maddy Wallace at the Gibson library. If that's you, this is yours." He gave a wide smile. "Merry Christmas."

"Thanks."

The basket sat on the corner of the desk and the little girl who was waiting for her library card looked at it eagerly. "Are you going to open it?"

"Do you think I should?" Maddy asked.

The girl nodded vigorously.

There was no one waiting in line, so Maddy untied

the ribbon and folded it carefully, then peeled back the plastic wrapping. Inside the basket was an assortment of her favorite things from the Daily Grind. There was a little pot with a built-in strainer for tea leaves, three small tins of different teas, a package of biscotti tied with a ribbon, a box of shortbread cookies, a bag of scone mix and four fresh pieces of strudel, the crisp pastry flaked with coarse sugar and with caramel and crimson fruit showing through the slits in the dough. Apple and cherry—her favorites.

And a little card. But she already knew what it was going to say.

"'To Maddy, from your secret Santa,'" she read aloud, shaking her head with amazement.

"That's lovely," said the girl's mother. "What a gorgeous basket."

Maddy beamed. "I've got a secret Santa this year. This is the third present I've received."

"What's a secret Santa?" the girl asked.

"Well, someone is giving me early Christmas presents, and they aren't telling me who they are. It's a mystery."

"I like mysteries."

Maddy looked at the assortment of books the girl had chosen to check out and smiled. "I see that. So, I've been looking at clues and I've been trying to figure out who my secret Santa is. I'm pretty sure it's my mom and dad. But it's nice getting surprises."

"Presents are always fun," she agreed.

In the basket were some assorted individual chocolates, and Maddy took one out and looked at the mom for approval. "Is a chocolate okay?" She nodded and

Maddy held it out. "I think sharing is fun, too. Would you like one?"

Her smile lit up the room. "Thanks."

"You're welcome." Maddy ran the plastic card through the scanner once more and activated it. "And now you have your very own library card. Keep this safe, okay?" She scanned the books' bar codes and handed them over. "When you finish them, come back and tell me what you think."

The girl nodded vigorously. Her mom leaned over and quietly said, "Thank you, Ms. Wallace. She's had a rough time with reading, and I'm trying to make it fun and find stuff she likes."

"Keep an eye on events, then," Maddy suggested. "In the new year we'll be starting up a new children's reading club, and there are always special activities over spring break and the summer."

"We will. And merry Christmas."

When they were gone, Maddy sneaked away to the break room and treated herself to one of the cherry strudels. The pastry melted in her mouth and she closed her eyes in appreciation. The tires had been practical and expensive; the tree was for the family. But this... this present was just for her, and a wonderful treat that she would never have splurged on for herself. After her crazy morning, it turned the day completely around.

With a quick glance at her phone, she realized she had about two minutes to make a call. She dialed the number quickly and her mom answered right away.

"I got the delivery," Maddy said. "It's wonderful."

"What delivery?"

"Come on, Mom, I know you and Dad are my secret Santa. The basket from the Grind is exactly what I would have wanted. Right down to my favorite kinds of tea. Only you could have known that."

"Honey, I'm glad you like it, but we're not your secret Santa."

She grinned. "You keep saying that. Anyway, fine, I won't bug you about it again. Just know that I love it and I love you both."

There was a light laugh at the other end. "We love you, too."

"I've gotta get back to work. Talk soon."

"Of course. 'Bye, sweetie."

When Maddy hung up, she knew there was nothing that could ruin her good mood.

SHE WAS WRONG.

Maddy finished work at six and rushed straight to the day care, where the boys were the last children to be picked up. Luke was crying and his nose was running, a sure sign of full-on teething, and Liam didn't look that happy, either—probably because his brother was miserable. Maddy got them home as quickly as possible and sat them in their high chairs while she heated some supper for them.

They'd just been fed and Maddy had taken a bite of the last leftover piece of cold fried chicken when Luke began to fuss and threw up. She hurried to clean up the mess—thank God it was in the kitchen and not on any carpet—and tried to soothe him, all the while herding Liam along to the tub. They both loved bath time and needed to be cleaned up, and once she got them in the warm water with some rubber ducks and frogs, she let out a big breath. Poor Luke's cheeks were bright red, and he grabbed the washcloth and shoved it in his mouth, sucking on it to ease the pain of his gums.

She couldn't keep them in the tub forever, though, and she got them into pajamas, put a fresh bib around Luke's neck to absorb the drool, and put a little more numbing gel on his gums. She could feel the hard bump of the tooth trying to poke through and felt terribly sorry for him, but it seemed his fussiness put everything off-kilter. Liam fell and hit his head, and his crying set off Luke again, and by the time she got them both settled in bed she was ready to sit down and have a right good cry herself.

When the phone rang, she grabbed it after the first ring so it wouldn't disturb the hard-won peace.

It was Cole.

"You sound tired. Busy night?"

"You might say that."

"I wondered how Luke was feeling. Still fussy?"

She sighed, leaning her head back against the sofa. "Yeah. He's got a tooth that's almost through."

"That doesn't sound like fun."

"For either of us. He threw up his supper, was clingy, Liam fell and bumped his head…"

"Sounds like you could use a break."

"Yeah. I think I'm going to go run myself a bath and go to bed. I have an eight-hour day tomorrow."

"The day care is okay with Luke being so out of sorts?"

"For the most part. I'll send stuff with him." While Cole's money was helpful, she didn't want to say that a day off work meant the loss of a whole day's pay. Even if most of it went to child care, it was a necessity.

"Well, sorry you had a rough day. If you need to miss your next morning here, don't worry about it."

She let out a relieved breath. She wouldn't take him up on it, but it was very understanding of him to offer. "Thank you, Cole."

"No problem. I hope you and the boys all feel better. Maybe you should make a cup of tea and just relax for a few hours."

She thought of the new tea in the basket in the kitchen and smiled. "I just got some new tea. Maybe I'll do that."

"I'll let you go, then. Oh, before I do, I had an idea today."

"What sort of idea?"

"Well, it'll depend on how the boys are feeling, of course. But I heard what you said about going on a date here in town and I think I found a compromise."

"You did?"

"The theater in Great Falls is showing *It's a Wonderful Life* on the weekend. I'll arrange for a sitter if you'll go with me Friday night."

She loved that movie. And a movie was fun but not overly intimate, and chances were they'd never see anyone they knew. But a sitter? Maddy was used to leaving the boys with the day care or her parents. She wasn't sure she trusted Cole to work out that detail. "Who did you have in mind to babysit?"

"A kid at a nearby ranch. Oldest of five and with tons

of experience. If they're free, of course. I haven't asked. I wanted to see if you'd say yes first."

She hesitated.

"Maddy, come to a movie with me. I'll buy you popcorn. Don't you deserve a night out?"

She was so tempted. She hadn't had a night out like that in so long. When she did have a chance to go out alone, she took it to run errands without having to drag car seats and diapers along. But a movie…and popcorn…and fun…

"If your babysitter is available. And you'll have to come early so I can make sure I'm comfortable leaving the boys."

"Of course." She could hear the smile in his voice. "So you're in? It's a date?"

Her heart gave a little flutter. "Yes, it's a date."

"Perfect. And now I'll let you get to your peace and quiet. Good night, Maddy."

"Good night, Cole."

She hung up the phone and sat in the silence for a few minutes, and then a smile spread across her face. Maybe she shouldn't be so excited, but she was. Between today's surprise gift and her Friday plans, she was starting to feel like a human being again.

As the week wore on, so did the glow. Luke's tooth came through, to everyone's relief, Maddy made it to Cole's as previously arranged, and she even managed to sneak a few hours of shopping and bought some adorable things for the boys for Christmas, as well as a lovely sweater and scarf for her mom and a DVD box set for her dad. On Thursday, during her afternoon shift, another delivery arrived at the library for her, and this time it was a present for the boys. She tore off the wrapping to discover a plush snowman and penguin, each about twelve inches high. Delighted, she pressed a button on the penguin's wing and he sang a song to the tune of "I'm a Little Teapot." She quickly turned it off again—it was abnormally loud in the quiet library— but she was enchanted just the same.

The card simply said, "To Luke and Liam, from Santa."

This really had to stop. But surely, with Christmas only a week away, the gifts would quit arriving.

She tucked the parcel under the desk, but there was no denying it. The Christmas spirit was definitely starting to catch hold.

Chapter Eleven

Cole tried not to be nervous as he arrived at Maddy's with sixteen-year-old Will Fletcher in the passenger seat. Fletch, as his friends called him, was tonight's babysitter. Cole had promised Maddy he'd look after the arrangements, and he had. And then they were going to Great Falls to a movie. Not just any movie, but a showing of *It's a Wonderful Life*. Cole figured if anything could give a boost of Christmas spirit, that was it.

"So, Maddy will give you the lowdown on the boys. They're great kids. Busy, but good."

Fletch looked over at Cole. "Dude, relax. I've been looking after my brothers and sisters for a long time. I got this."

"Right. I know that."

"You got some nerves, bro?"

Cole gave a short chuckle. Was he going to get dating advice from a kid now? This was what his life had come to—picking up babysitters and getting love life advice. Maybe Tanner was right. If he'd been seeing anyone else, he would have bailed by now. But he hadn't. He was still trying. And that was both encouraging and scary as hell.

"Maybe a few," he admitted.

"Just keep it chill. She's a mom, right? Just having a night out without kids is a big deal. Believe me, I've heard my mom say it enough." Fletch rolled his eyes. "Which is why I started babysitting as soon as I was old enough. Happy Mom equals more good stuff for me."

Cole chuckled. "Sounds like you have it all figured out."

"Not hardly. Right now moms are easier to figure out than sixteen-year-old girls, know what I mean?"

"Amen, brother." Cole turned off the car and took the keys out of the ignition. "All right, let's go."

The walkway was lit up with the twinkly lights he'd installed, and he could see the tree through the front window. When he got to the front door, he knocked and stepped back.

When she opened the door, he caught his breath.

It wasn't that she'd dressed up in her finest. She was wearing black trousers and a red top that seemed to gather beneath her breasts before flowing down over her waist and hips. He'd seen lots of women wear the same sort of outfit to work around town, but on Maddy it looked different. Special. A delicate necklace lay at her throat, and she'd pulled her hair back from the sides and curled the rest in big, tumbling curls.

She'd made an effort. As if tonight was an occasion. And it was. Their first real, official date where they went somewhere and he paid and...yeah. This was the real thing.

"Hi," she said simply, and smiled, and his world turned upside down.

"Hi," Fletch said, holding out his hand. "I'm Fletch, your babysitter for tonight."

"You are?"

"Yes, ma'am."

Cole finally found his tongue. "Sorry. Right. This is Will Fletcher. He's got lots of babysitting experience, don't worry. Plus the boys might like playing with another guy, right?"

"My brother always liked to get all his cars together and play smash-up derby," Fletch joked.

"Well, come in. I'll introduce you to the twins, show you where everything is."

She stood aside to let them in, showed Fletch where to hang his coat and watched as he went straight to the living room, where the boys were playing. "Are you sure about this?" she asked, her eyes worried.

"You mean because he's a guy? Positive. His family lives close to the ranch, and he's the oldest of five. He's looked after his siblings lots and gave me references for other babysitting jobs. The boys are going to be fine, Maddy."

"And I'll have my cell."

"That's right. And we're not that far away, either. He seems to be making himself at home."

They looked over. Sure enough, they were playing farm with the animals and the boys had taken right to him. He sat on the floor, legs crossed, and Luke ran over and shoved a horse into his hands.

"I should give him the rundown so we won't be late."

"That'd be good." Cole smiled down at her. "But before you do that…"

He reached for her hand and made sure she was looking at him. "You look really pretty tonight, Maddy."

A blush colored her cheeks. "Thanks. I'll be right back."

He took a seat in a chair as she went over contact numbers and routines with Fletch, showed him the boys' room and where everything was. "If there's any trouble, just text me. We're going to a movie, but I'll keep my phone on vibrate."

"We'll be fine. We're going to have fun, right, guys?" He looked at her and grinned. "Though I'll admit, I might have trouble telling them apart."

She laughed. "A lot of people do at first. Liam's a little shyer than Luke, and Luke's a tad bigger."

"Got it."

"And you've got all my numbers?"

"Yes, ma'am."

"In bed by eight, okay?"

Fletch nodded and Cole admired his patience. "Eight sharp. Go have fun."

Cole held her coat as she shrugged it on and then put on heeled knee-high boots that made his mouth water, they were so sexy. "Ready?"

She let out a deep breath. "Ready."

They escaped outside into the cold air and Cole held her elbow as they went down the walk, just in case there was any ice. At the truck he opened her door and shut it again after she hopped up. When he was inside he started the engine and cranked on the heater. "I think winter is definitely here to stay," he remarked.

"Me, too."

As she fastened her seat belt, he casually observed, "New lights on the hedges. Nice."

"Mom and Dad strike again," she said lightly, smiling. "They really went crazy this week. I got a basket at work and then the cutest plush animals for the boys, and I came home from work yesterday to this. I could get used to having a secret Santa."

"I bet." He smiled back. She was enjoying being spoiled a little bit, and she deserved it. And if she never knew it was him, it didn't matter. He loved Christmas, and knowing he'd made hers a little more fun was all the thanks he needed.

"I do feel a little guilty, though," she said with a sigh. "It seems pretty one-sided."

"But that's probably why it's a secret. Knowing would take the fun out of it, wouldn't it?"

"Maybe." She shrugged as they backed out of the driveway and started down the street. "But at this point it's just a technicality. They keep saying they aren't doing it, but I know it's them."

Once they hit the highway it was just the two of them and the songs on the radio. It felt strange, going somewhere alone. They hadn't, not since the day he'd run into her and they'd gone for coffee. He'd gotten used to the boys being around, and now he felt a gap of silence with their absence.

"It feels funny without the kids," he commented.

She smiled. "I know. Sometimes I think I'm going to

have to have them surgically removed." A light laugh followed. "This is really nice, Cole. Thanks for asking me."

"It seemed a fair compromise." He grinned. "Besides, you, me, in a dark movie theater? Hard to complain about that."

"Cole!" She looked over at him. "I haven't made out in a movie theater in over ten years, and I'm not about to revisit that activity."

He laughed and put a hand over his heart. "Don't worry. I'll be the soul of gentlemanly behavior."

As much as it killed him, he would.

They spent the rest of the drive into Great Falls talking about the holidays, what was going on around town and his parents' vacation, which was rapidly coming to a close. "Are you still coming over on Sunday to decorate the tree?"

"Of course, if you still want me to."

"You know I do."

He pulled into the parking lot, which was already filling up. "Well, here we are. Let's go get our tickets and a big tub of popcorn."

He held her hand as they crossed the lot to the doors. The theater was a popular spot on a Friday night, and after they bought their tickets and concessions, they discovered the seats were filling up fast. The top rows were completely packed, and the best seats left were about a third of the way up. Closer to the screen than Cole liked, but it would have to do. They made their way down the row and took turns holding food while they hung their coats over the seats.

"I don't remember the last time I went to a movie," Maddy said, settling into her seat and reaching for her soda. "Over a year for sure. Probably over two."

"Me, either," Cole admitted. When he did go, black-and-white holiday films were last on his list of must-watches.

But this year he was Santa Claus. And he'd known it was something she'd like.

The lights dimmed and he saw Maddy smiling at him as the screen came to life with current previews.

"Do you know I've never actually seen *It's a Wonderful Life*?" he whispered, leaning over.

"What? Really?" She took a drink of her soda and looked so very young. "But it's a classic."

He shrugged. "That every-time-a-bell-rings stuff never made me want to."

"So why now?"

He didn't answer. Just looked into her eyes and held her gaze. Watched her expression soften as she understood. For her. He was doing it for her.

"You're going to love it," she whispered and turned to face the front fully before reaching into the tub for a handful of hot, buttery popcorn.

She was right, he did enjoy it. It wasn't anything like he expected, and Jimmy Stewart's lovable comedy was perfect. Near the end, when everyone was parading through the house giving back to the man who'd always sacrificed for Bedford Falls, he looked over and saw Maddy sniffling and wiping her eyes. He smiled, feeling an unexpected tenderness in the moment, and handed her a napkin. She gave him a rueful smile, then dabbed at her tears. The popcorn bucket had been put on the floor long ago, and Cole reached over and took her hand in his, rubbing his thumb over hers.

It was a far cry from making out, but there was something about it just the same, something that reached in and confirmed something he'd suspected all along: Maddy Wallace was different.

She was worth it.

As the credits started rolling, he looked over at her. She looked back, and they gazed at each other for several long moments as the crowd began to filter out. It wasn't until another couple said, "Excuse me," edging past them to the end of the row, that they broke eye contact and hurried to stand up and let the people pass. The moment gone, they put on their coats and gloves and prepared to make their way out into the cold again.

"Did you want to do something else?" he asked as they made their way outside.

"I should probably get home. I don't leave the boys with someone new very often."

"Did Fletch call or text?"

She shook her head. "No."

"Then let's go get a coffee. Or hot chocolate or something. It's early. It's only nine thirty."

"Okay."

Once more he opened her door, closed it, got in and started the truck. But there was a different feeling than he'd had before. Bigger, scarier, amazing. After all this time, he figured he'd better face the truth. He'd done a lot of soul-searching after talking to his brother, and the conclusion he'd reached was that it was possible he was falling in love. With the most complicated woman in Gibson. Wasn't that just a kick in the pants?

Falling in love. That was so not what he'd intended when he'd started all this. It scared the hell out of him and felt amazing and exciting all at the same time.

Before leaving the parking lot, he slid across the seat and cupped her face in his hands. "I've been waiting over two hours to do this," he murmured, and then he kissed her.

Despite her misgivings about being in public, Maddy didn't hold back much. He kept the kiss decent, of course, and kept his hands where they should be in public. But that didn't mean there wasn't a wealth of passion and longing in that one kiss. "You sure you want to go for coffee?" he asked breathlessly. "We could go parking like a couple of teenagers."

She laughed against his mouth. "Coffee," she said, kissing the corner of his mouth. "All we'd need is to get caught by some cop making out in your truck."

"Damn," he muttered. But he grinned, anyway.

He drove them to a little coffee shop near the highway and they ordered peppermint hot chocolates instead of something loaded with caffeine. Maddy took a sip and licked whipped cream off her upper lip. "Cole, do you suppose we're getting old, worrying about drinking caffeine at night?" Her smile was impish and anything but old.

"Naw. We're wise. Besides, we both have to get up early in the morning."

She nodded. "Yeah. Responsibilities."

He reached across the table and took her hand. "Do

you ever wish you were eighteen again, with everything before you?"

Maddy lifted her cup, took another drink and paused before answering. "Sometimes I miss having the freedom to just pick up and go somewhere, you know? But honestly? Despite everything, I wouldn't trade those two boys for any do-overs."

He smiled. "I know. They're pretty special."

"It doesn't scare you, that I have kids?"

Cole met her gaze. "Scare me? No. Make me be careful? Oh, yes. Dating a single mom is serious business."

He took a drink of his cocoa, rich chocolate and bright peppermint. Maddy laughed and wiped his lip with a napkin. "So in your estimation, we're dating?" she asked.

Why did that particular question make his stomach knot up with nerves, as if he was seventeen again? "Aren't we? Let's see. We've had coffee—twice now—and we've taken a wagon ride in the snow. Then there's dinner, and Christmas tree decorating, and a movie. In the space of about three weeks. What would you call it?"

Her cheeks pinkened. "Dating."

"Maddy," he said quietly, understanding all too well where she was coming from. "I know you want to keep things low-key in Gibson. But eventually people are going to figure it out."

"I know. I know," she repeated meaningfully. "Just not yet, okay?"

"Okay."

"That's it?"

He shrugged. "Sure." Then he smiled. "For now, anyway."

They finished their cocoa and it was ten thirty by the time they hit the road for Gibson. When they got home, the porch light was on and so were the Christmas lights, but the house seemed quiet. They found Fletch in the living room, watching something on TV. Every toy was picked up and put away and she didn't see any dirty dishes, either. Definite bonus points for the sitter.

"Hi," she said quietly. "Any troubles?"

Fletch turned off the TV and stretched. "Well, eight was more like eight thirty by the time I got them to settle down, but nothing since then. They really like playing with that farm, don't they?"

Maddy nodded. "Thanks, Will."

"I'll give you a ride home," Cole said, nodding. "Here's the keys. I'll be right out."

Fletch gave him a knowing smile but hastened to put on his coat and shoes. "'Bye, Ms. Wallace. Anytime you need a sitter, let me know."

"Thanks, Will, I'll do that."

Fletch slid outside and the lights of the truck lit up the driveway as he turned on the engine.

"So," Cole said, wishing he had all night, but knowing that it was probably better that he had to drive Fletch home. "I guess this is where we say good-night."

"I had a really good time," she said quietly, turning her soft eyes up at him.

"Me, too."

The kiss this time seemed as natural as snowflakes falling to the ground. Their lips met easily, with a growing familiarity.

"I'll see you on Sunday, then?" he asked, wishing

he could find an excuse to see her tomorrow but realizing she had to work.

"Sunday. Why don't I bring lunch over for you and Tanner?"

"That'd be great. Can I have a couple of these for dessert?" He kissed her again, thinking she tasted sweeter than any candy cane or cookie.

"Fletch is going to know exactly what we're doing."

"Well, I would hope so, or I'll have to give that boy an education."

She laughed. "Go. I'll see you Sunday."

"'Bye, sweetheart." He leaned forward and kissed her forehead, and then ducked out the door.

Yep, he was in big trouble. And the greatest part was that he didn't even really seem to mind. Maybe it was truly time for him to move forward and take the next step. The fact that he was taking that step with pretty, gentle Maddy just made it that much sweeter.

Chapter Twelve

"Beef stew coming through," Maddy called out as she entered the warm house.

"We're in here," Tanner replied from the living room. She looked over and saw that he and Cole had already put the tree in its stand. So much for Tanner being jealous. Their tree was at least a foot taller than hers, and fuller, too, to accommodate the larger room and higher ceiling.

She put the slow cooker on the table. "Be right back. I've got to get the boys."

She went to the door, but Cole stepped inside with a boy on each arm and the diaper bag over his shoulder. "Looking for these?"

"I was just going to get them. Thanks, Cole."

"No problem. I saw you drive in from the barn. Here you go, slugger." He handed Liam to Maddy and then put Luke on the floor and started undoing his snowsuit. Together they got the boys undressed and soon the pair was standing in the middle of the kitchen with twisted socks and hair sticking up at odd angles.

"They've already eaten, so let me get them settled

with some toys and we can eat, too." She busied herself plugging in the slow cooker to make sure everything was hot, then reached for the bag, taking out a variety of toys.

"I found something when I was looking for the decorations," Cole said. "The old VHS movies Mom had for us when we were little. Including Christmas ones. I can put one on for them."

She laughed. "You mean you still have a VCR?"

"Yeah, I found that in the attic, too, and it still works." He grinned as if he was immensely proud of himself. "We have an assortment of classics. Rudolph, Frosty, Charlie Brown and the Grinch."

His face looked so boyishly excited about it all that she said, "Pick your favorite. We'll start there."

The boys wandered around the living room, familiar now with the lower level of the house, while Cole set up the video and Maddy got out dishes and put the buns she'd brought on a plate. The television was larger than hers, and as soon as the Charlie Brown music came on, the twins' attention was grabbed. Between that and the toys, Maddy figured she had about twenty minutes to eat before she'd have to referee something.

They all sat down to beef stew and crusty buns and the mood was definitely festive. The warm feelings from Friday night's date had stayed with her all weekend long. She liked being with Cole—liked it a lot. As she split a bun and buttered it, she listened to him tease Tanner about some girl he'd been seeing. Cole was sweet to her and so good and patient with the boys.

Dating hadn't really been on her radar, but she wasn't sorry. As long as he was content to take it slow.

She still didn't quite trust herself yet. Her mood took a little dip as she remembered how happy she'd been before. She'd been so sure things were great only to find out she'd been wrong all along. It was going to take a while for her to get past that.

But if Cole could be as patient with her as he was with the boys...

"You got quiet all of a sudden," Cole observed.

"Oh. Sorry. Just thinking."

"I've heard it's bad to do too much of that," Tanner said, grinning.

"You could stand to do a little more," Cole shot back at his brother, a crooked smile on his face.

"Yeah, yeah. Someday I might surprise you all," Tanner said, scooping up some stew. "This is really good, Maddy."

"Thanks. It's my mom's recipe."

Maddy had barely scraped the bottom of her bowl when the kids started winding up. As she tended to them, Tanner and Cole took over tidying the lunch mess. Then Maddy put in another video—as much for Cole as for the boys—and cuddled with them on the sofa as Cole and Tanner debated over the lights for the tree.

Her heart hurt a bit, listening to them bicker good-naturedly. It felt like a real family moment, only this wasn't her family. It was lovely to be included, and of course she cared for Cole. How could she not? But it wasn't the same.

Why was she so melancholy today, anyway? Hadn't

she promised herself to live in the present? She let out a deep breath, trying to send her negativity with it. Her beautiful sons were snuggled up on her lap, a Christmas movie was playing, she was with friends decorating their tree. She had way too much to be thankful for.

Rudolph was nearly done by the time the lights were perfect, and both boys had fallen asleep. Maddy eased them down on to the sofa and covered them with one of Ellen's crocheted afghans, pausing a moment to study their little faces. How she loved them…even when they made her tired and crazy. Looking at them as they slept chased away all the bad things.

Cole came over and looped his arms around her from behind, surprising her. "They're pretty cute, huh."

"Cole, your brother's here."

"Tanner's not stupid. He knows we've been seeing each other."

Somehow the embrace felt like more, though. Simply because it was in the presence of someone else. "It's just new, that's all," she whispered.

"You'll get used to it. I'm a hugger."

She couldn't stop the smile that touched her lips. "I'll keep that in mind."

"Okay, lovebirds, I've got some stuff over here I have no idea what to do with."

Maddy knew she was blushing a little when she turned back. Tanner was holding rolls of gold mesh in his hands, looking a little helpless. She laughed. "You want some help?"

"Please," he said. "Our mom usually does this part."

She took the mesh from his hands and played with it

for a few moments, getting the feel of it in her fingers. "Okay. I'm going to start here." She went to the top and back of the tree. "Is there a step stool or something?"

Cole brought her the stool and she climbed up, then twisted the wire mesh and anchored it to a branch. "Tanner, unroll this as I go so I have some slack to work with." She handed him the roll and they made their way around the tree, with Maddy making puffs with the mesh before gathering it around a branch. It was finicky work, and it took a good amount of time and some joking around to get it done, but in the end the gigantic tree was adorned with what looked like lovely gold ribbon. Their tree had white lights instead of multicolored, and the effect was stunning.

"Wow," Cole said, admiring. "That looks good. I think we should say that we did it ourselves, Tanner." He nudged Maddy's elbow.

"Mom will never believe it," Tanner said.

"You're right."

They were in the middle of putting on the ornaments when Tanner's cell rang. He answered and Maddy heard Tanner say he'd be right there. When he hung up, Cole asked, "What's going on?"

"Jimmy's on call this weekend, but his car won't start. We've got a run to the hospital."

"Accident?"

Tanner went to the closet and took out his EMT jacket. "Baby's coming. Hopefully we'll have lots of time to get to the hospital. The roads are good."

Maddy's blood ran cold for a moment, but then she told herself it was silly. The only reason she was thinking of Laura was because Laura was the only pregnant woman she knew. But then, she was due around Christmastime and the holiday was only a few days away... coincidence?

"Who is it?" Cole asked, and Maddy held her breath.

Tanner had the grace to look uncomfortable. "It's Laura Jessup."

Maddy could feel Cole's gaze on her. She refused to look at him right now, instead taking the ornament in her hand and hanging it on the tree with calm precision.

"You'd better get going, then," Cole said, and no one spoke as Tanner dressed and headed out the door.

"Are you okay?" Cole asked quietly.

"I don't know," Maddy answered honestly. She reached for another ornament and hung it, not knowing what else to do but needing to keep her hands busy.

"I'm sorry I asked. I never thought about Laura..."

"The problem is, I think about her too often." She picked up another ornament and looked for an empty space to hang it. "She's having my husband's baby."

"Maddy, do you know that for sure?"

She turned on him then, annoyed with his placating tone. "The rumors have been around for months and not once has she denied it. Come on, Cole. If you were accused of having an affair with a married man and carrying his child, and it wasn't true, don't you think you'd clear the air?"

Cole didn't say anything.

She tossed the ornament she was holding back into the box. "I'm sorry. I didn't mean to ruin a nice afternoon. I know I promised to live in the present. But it's hard when reminders of the past sneak up to slap me in the face, you know?"

"Sure."

His brief agreement only made her more annoyed. "You think I'm being unreasonable."

His jaw hardened. "What I think is that I want you to move past this so we might have a chance at something great. Because I really care for you, Maddy. More than I expected to."

Oh, Lord. Her emotions were already a disaster zone, and adding his feelings to it only made it worse. She didn't know what to think or say. On one hand, knowing he cared for her felt so good, but on the other hand, it only added to the pressure.

She took a step back. "Cole, I told you I needed to go slowly."

"I know. But there's slow and then there's slow, and I've really been trying here. I tell myself to just be a friend. A good neighbor. That neither of us is ready, but honest to God, Maddy, every time we're together I feel like I'm falling in—"

"Don't say it." She cut him off. "Just don't. We've been out together a handful of times over the course of a month. Not even."

He went to her and grabbed her forearm. "It's more than that. You know it. There's something real between us. Something awesome, and I'm willing to name it. But I can't keep fighting against a ghost. Surely you can see that, right?"

She was starting to feel overwhelmed. Over on the sofa, the boys slept soundly. They'd lost their father.

Right now Tanner was on his way to help bring their half brother or sister into the world. Did Cole not understand how hard that was for her to bear? Did he want her to pretend that it had never happened? That it wasn't happening right now? Impossible.

"Look," she said, trying to remain calm. "There *is* something between us. But I can't just turn my feelings on and off. And I can't just snap my fingers and say I'm over it. Don't you think I would if I could?" Her heart hurt just saying the words. "Don't you get that Gavin and I said vows and then they turned out to be meaningless for him? How could I have been so wrong about him? How can I ever be sure of anyone again?"

"What are you saying?" He pressed on, staying in front of her, not letting her escape the conversation. "Are you saying that there's never a chance for us because you don't trust me?"

"I don't trust anyone, don't you see?" she blurted out.

She looked into Cole's eyes, saw the hurt register there and felt terrible about it. She lowered her voice. "Cole, I've enjoyed being with you. It's been wonderful in so many ways. But when I said baby steps, I really meant it."

He swallowed, his Adam's apple bobbing. "I know that, so I tried to show you in any way I could. I didn't want to use words, and so I tried to show you with my actions. Why else would I have done all the secret Santa stuff? And I really started caring for the boys and—"

"Wait. *You're* my secret Santa?" Something inside her froze at the knowledge. "It wasn't my parents?"

As if he sensed he'd put his foot in it, he spoke carefully. "I…swore them to secrecy. They were in on it and so was Tanner."

Maddy turned away. The tires. The Christmas tree. The lights on the hedge and the gift basket at work. The presents for the boys. That had all been Cole, in addition to paying her for the scant amount of housework she'd done here. And the dates themselves…dinner, movies, coffee…

"Wow," she said quietly, taking a step back. "I must have seemed really pathetic to you."

"Of course not! Maddy, come on…"

She held up a hand. "That first night at the library, when you wanted to stay and help, I should have known. Poor Maddy Wallace, with two babies and no husband. You know, for a while I wondered if you asked me out because you like a challenge. But that's not it, is it? You've got a rescue complex. You want to swoop in and fix everything. Well, here's a news flash, Cole. I don't need to be rescued. And I sure as hell don't need to be fixed. The boys and I were managing fine on our own."

She must have touched a nerve, because instead of the imploring expression he'd had before, he was starting to look angry. His lips thinned and his eyebrows knit together as he frowned at her. "Have you been talking to Tanner?"

She frowned, confused. "Of course not. Except when you were both here. Why would you ask that?"

"Because he asked me the same damned thing in almost those exact words. You want to know why I did the Santa thing? Because I knew damn well that you wouldn't accept help any other way."

"Maybe I didn't *want* the help."

"Maddy," he said, and his tone said clearly, *Don't be ridiculous*. Which only added fuel to both her temper and her humiliation.

"So this job…it really was made-up, then. You didn't need me…"

"Could we have managed around here? Sure. But having you here has helped out a lot. I told you it was mutually beneficial."

"I want to know and I want you to answer me honestly," she demanded. "Did you come up with this job as a way of helping me without it being 'charity'?"

He didn't answer right away, which was answer enough.

"You wanted to give the boys a good Christmas," he defended.

She closed her eyes. "Not at the expense of my pride."

"Pride can be overrated."

"Not when you've had yours taken away." Tears pricked her eyelids. "I had so little pride left, Cole. And good intentions or not, you took more of it away from me. I felt guilty enough thinking it was my parents helping out, but I figured there'd come a time when I could repay the favor. They're my folks. But this…"

She sighed heavily. "You went behind my back. You lied because you knew I wouldn't accept the truth. How can you possibly think that would be okay after what I've been through?"

He stared at her as though she were crazy. "You're mad at me because I helped. Ouch."

"I'm mad at you because you went behind my back! How am I supposed to trust you after this?"

Cole swore and ran his hand over his hair. "For God's sake, Maddy, that's crazy. I played Santa Claus and you're making it out to be a capital crime. I helped out a friend who was having a hard time making ends meet, and I did it in secret because I knew she'd hate feeling like it was charity. So sue me for caring and trying to help! You know what? I don't think the problem is that you don't trust me. I think you do. I think you have feelings for me just as much as I do for you. And I think that scares you to death, because the person you really don't trust is yourself. You don't trust your own judgment and so this is the perfect excuse to drive me away."

Her mouth dropped open. "That's ridiculous." But even as she said the words she knew she was wrong. Hadn't she just been thinking the same thing only minutes ago?

"Is it? Every time we get close, either you pull back or I do so I don't push you further than you want to go. You're very careful to only give little pieces of yourself. Maybe I did like the feeling of helping you and seeing the smile light up your face. But you know what? I can't wait around forever for a person who's only going to ration out their affection according to how afraid they are at the moment. I've done that before, and in the end I was the one sitting there alone."

"I knew it would come to this. The whole take-it-slowly thing never works. Someone always wants more…"

"I'm not asking for much."

"You're asking for everything."

Once more silence fell over the room.

Cole met her gaze. There was sadness in his eyes, she thought with a bit of wonder. And inevitability. She almost wished she could take back the words, but she couldn't, and besides, they'd been the truth.

The truth.

"You're not ready for everything," he murmured. "Even if I wanted to give it to you. And now I realize you might never be. You loved Gavin and he betrayed that trust. For the rest of your life you're going to look at a man and ask yourself one question—do I believe the words coming out of his mouth?"

"Cole."

He shook his head. "Maddy, you are sweet, and kind, and hardworking. You're a wonderful mother and your boys…they're a little crazy and a whole lot cute. You're beautiful and I know you stopped me from saying it before, but I'm pretty sure I've fallen in love with you. I didn't expect it. You just had a way of making me want to make your life better. To see you smile more. Maybe I went about it the wrong way, I don't know. All I know is the thought of the three of you sharing Christmas with me has been on my mind for a while now. I want to see the boys' faces Christmas morning when they open their presents. I want to kiss you under the mistletoe again and drink Christmas morning coffee with you. I've never, ever said that to another woman, Maddy. Never."

She felt as though her heart was weeping, and what he said must have been true, because tears streaked down her face. "But we never made Christmas plans…" It was a dumb thing to say, but at such a moment she didn't know what to say. She was so full of conflicting emotions nothing seemed clear.

"I wanted to. I wanted you three to spend Christmas Eve here and maybe I could share Christmas morning with you."

"My parents are coming over Christmas morning." It would have meant making their relationship official to her folks.

"I know," he answered, and she knew that had been his intention all along.

He was asking too much. As heartrending as his plea was, she simply wasn't ready. "I can't," she murmured. "I'm sorry, Cole. I've enjoyed these last few weeks, but you want more than I can give. You always have. And I can't escape the feeling that somehow you bought your way in." She held up a hand when he started to protest. "Oh, I know you didn't intend it that way. I do respect you enough to believe that. But you weren't honest, and that's the one thing I need."

"Let me be honest now, then. I love you, Maddy."

She hated that she couldn't say the words back. And it wasn't that she didn't care. She did. So much. Things wouldn't have progressed this far if she didn't. But it was a long way to love and the kind of relationship he was looking for.

"I'm sorry, Cole," she answered, and to her chagrin she saw his jaw muscle tighten for just a second before he took a breath and let it out.

"Me, too," he replied, turning away.

There was a charged silence and then Maddy knew

she had to go. "I'd better get the boys together and head home."

"Let them sleep out their nap. I can leave..."

He'd leave his own house rather than stay a moment longer. She couldn't blame him. She wished she could give him what he wanted. Wished it with all her heart. Instead she went to the kitchen and gathered up her things, then gently dressed the boys in their snowsuits for the drive home. On the tires he'd bought. To the house with the lights he'd put up and the tree he'd had delivered.

No matter what he said, she still felt like one big charity case.

"I'll help you take everything to the car," he said quietly.

"Thanks."

It was a quiet and sad procession they made to her car. She put the slow cooker and bag in the front, buckled the boys in the back and was about to get in the driver's side when Cole reached for her arm and pulled her back.

"Maddy," he said, his voice rough with emotion. "Tell me what to do and I'll do it. I'm not giving up on us."

She wrenched her arm away, choking on a sob. "Don't, Cole. Please. Just let me go."

She got in and shut the door, started the car. And as she drove away she saw him in the rearview mirror, looking about as lonely as she'd ever seen a man.

She'd done that. She had. She'd hurt him terribly. And that was the last thing she wanted to do.

Maddy had heaped a fair bit of criticism on herself

over the past months, but today she was as bad a person as she'd ever felt. And she was the only one to blame this time. She was the one running scared.

COLE SAT ON the sofa and put his head in his hands. Well. He'd definitely botched that up. What had he been thinking, saying that he loved her? Telling her about his ridiculous fantasy of spending Christmas together?

It was all true, though. That was the real kicker. Every single thing he'd said had been true.

The cushions were still warm from where Luke and Liam had been sleeping, and Cole sighed. If he were honest, those little guys had wormed their way into his heart, too. Today when he'd opened the car door, their little faces had lit up, and Liam, always a bit more reserved than Luke, had put his arms up first. They were pretty special kids. So was their mama, but he'd said the *L* word and she'd panicked.

He didn't realize how long he'd been sitting there until Tanner came in the door, stomping his feet. "Hey," he greeted. "Tree's all up. Where's Maddy and the boys? I figured they'd still be here."

Cole looked up at him and Tanner's face fell. "Shit. What happened?"

"I fell in love with her, that's what happened," Cole said. "I know, you don't have to say it. It's only been a few weeks. She mentioned that several times. And she went ballistic when she found out I was her secret Santa."

"She's got a lot of pride," Tanner said. He went to the fridge and grabbed two beers, popped the tops and went to sit by Cole, handing him one of the bottles. "And I'm guessing she found out in the middle of an argument rather than a *guess what?* moment."

Cole chuckled a little. He loved his little brother. Who else could make him laugh at a time like this? "Yeah. You're right."

"So are you just giving up?"

"She's not over her ex. Or at least, what he did to her. I wish she could see that I'm not him. That I wouldn't do that."

"Yeah, but she probably thought the same thing about Gavin. And that's the problem."

"I know. Dammit, I know."

"I'm sorry, Cole. I know you felt differently about her."

He nodded. "I've never told another woman that I loved her."

"What?" Tanner stared at him. "First of all, never? Not even Roni?"

Cole shook his head. "Roni asked me not to. Long story." One that had more to do with what she'd heard and seen at home than wanting to go slow. In her house, *I love you* had been an excuse, not an endearment.

"Wow. And you actually told Maddy that today?" He slapped himself in the forehead. "No wonder she took off."

"It's so bad to say *I love you* to a woman?"

Tanner shook his head. "Most women, when you're dating, are dying for you to be the one to say it first. But as you said, Maddy's different. And you haven't been seeing each other that long. She probably freaked."

"She did."

Tanner took a swig of beer; Cole did the same.

"Maybe you can just give her some time. She'll come around."

Cole wanted to take encouragement from the words, but he wasn't feeling very optimistic. "She was mad at me on so many levels that I think the ship has sailed. It's really over."

"I'm sorry," Tanner said quietly, and for a few minutes they simply sat, nursing their beers and thinking.

"By the way," Cole finally said, "what happened with Laura?"

"She'd waited awhile to call us, and by the time we got out there and to the hospital, the baby was crowning. She was delivered right in the emergency room. A healthy little girl."

A girl. Gavin's daughter, in all likelihood. Cole thought for a minute about how that would make Maddy feel in years to come. The little girl would be a year behind her brothers in school. They'd meet on the street. There would always, always be a reminder of his infidelity.

He'd pushed too hard and expected too much. Maybe he'd been particularly blessed, and while he was a whiz at helping out, maybe he wasn't so good at empathizing. All this time he'd blamed Roni for taking so much from him and leaving him with nothing in return, but maybe he hadn't been blameless, either. As Tanner had said when they'd been out riding, maybe helping so much sent a message that he didn't think she could manage on her own, and as a result he'd pushed Roni away. He'd pushed both of them away.

Maddy had surely humbled him today.

Tanner looked at Cole, his expression guarded. "I hope you don't mind me saying, but Laura reminded me a lot of Maddy."

"Don't tell Maddy that. She'll flip her lid."

Tanner let out a soft laugh. "Anyway, what I'm saying is that it's got to take some guts to bring a child into the world all on your own. And she knows what they say around town."

"Makes you wonder why she stays."

Tanner shrugged. "It's home. She probably has her reasons, which are none of our business. Sometimes people are stronger than we give them credit for, Cole."

"I know. My intentions came from a good place, you know what I mean?"

"Then give it some time and tell her that. You're not just going to give up, are you?"

Cole didn't know. Maddy had seemed pretty sure of herself when she left.

After a while they turned on the TV and looked for a hockey or football game. Tanner got up and put on a few steaks for supper, his specialty; Cole threw some frozen fries in the oven. Tomorrow their parents would be back, then it would be Christmas Eve, and Christmas Day.

He'd been looking forward to it this year, but not so much now. Not when the people he really wanted to be with were across town in their own house.

Chapter Thirteen

The library was open until 2:00 p.m. on Christmas Eve, and Maddy was scheduled to work. The boys were at her parents'; they'd bring them over later once Maddy was done with her errands. She'd forgotten croutons for the salad for dinner, and she'd made a pie for dessert and forgotten the ice cream. In fact she'd been forgetting things for the last two days. All because Cole Hudson had told her he loved her.

Well, he was a fool.

There wasn't much traffic at the library, either, which made her shift drag on endlessly. A few people came in to check out books for the holidays; a few more brought books back so they wouldn't be overdue during the break when the library was closed. Maddy was more than ready to leave when two o'clock came and she could lock the doors and log off the computers. They wouldn't open again until the twenty-seventh, so she went through and made sure everything was secure and turned off before leaving.

Cole's final pay to her was in an envelope in her purse. She wasn't sure whether she could spend it or not.

She felt guilty taking it now. She was still deliberating when she parked between the grocery store and the drugstore. And she was so preoccupied that she didn't hear the female voice calling her name until it was too late.

"Maddy. Madison. Madison Wallace."

When she finally clued in, she saw Laura Jessup bearing down on her, on her way out of the drugstore. Good Lord, was she out of the hospital already? There was nowhere to run. Maddy simply froze, feeling like the proverbial deer caught in the headlights.

Laura was carrying the baby in a carrier against her chest, underneath her jacket. *Gavin's baby*, Maddy realized, and her knees felt a little bit wobbly.

"Maddy," Laura said again, finally arriving, a little out of breath. Maddy noticed she wasn't wearing a speck of makeup and her hair was pulled into a hasty ponytail.

"You're out of the hospital already?" Maddy asked, not knowing what else to say.

"They sent me home this morning, so I could be home for Christmas."

"Oh."

God, could this be any more awkward...

"Look, Maddy, I've wanted to talk to you for a long time, but I got the feeling you weren't ready."

Maddy gave her a sharp look. "I don't think I'll ever be ready." She was all too aware of the baby, who seemed so very tiny. How was it possible she'd forgotten how small newborns were? All she could really see was a pink hat peeking out from beneath Laura's jacket. A girl. Something twisted inside her, thinking of Gavin having a daughter.

"I know. Which is why I figured, when I saw you, that now is as good a time as any. Maddy, you need to know the truth."

"No, I don't want to hear the details. Please, spare me that." Maddy wanted to run away, but the lot was packed with last-minute shoppers. A few were giving them funny looks. But the cart corral was on one side of her, her car on the other, and Laura in front. To escape she'd literally have to turn tail and run.

"That's just it. There are no details."

Maddy scoffed. "After all this time, you haven't denied a thing. Now you honestly expect me to believe that you and Gavin never had an affair? Is that what you're saying?" She stared pointedly at the lump of pink beneath Laura's jacket, and had a perverse urge to want to see the baby's face, to find out if she bore any resemblance to Gavin's family.

Laura's face reddened. "Maddy, just give me two minutes and hear me out."

Her expression was so earnest, so desperate, that Maddy paused. Maybe they needed to have this conversation. Maybe it was one of the things keeping her from moving forward. Either way, she found herself reluctantly agreeing. "Two minutes, Laura."

Relief showed on the other woman's face, and her right hand was pressed against the bundle inside her jacket. "I'm going to trust you with something. Something I trusted Gavin with, and I know he loved you something fierce."

"Don't presume to tell me about my husband," Maddy replied acidly.

"He did love you," she insisted, "and he said so all the time. He was helping me because I was an old friend. Nothing more. The only secrets we shared were because of lawyer-client privilege."

"Then the baby? How do you explain her?" Maddy looked down at the bundle sleeping beneath the jacket and instantly felt guilty. It wasn't the baby's fault that she was caught in the middle of all this ugliness.

"If I tell you, I need your word you won't tell anyone," she said. "Maddy, I know you hate me. But I need you to promise me this. You do and I know you'll understand."

Maddy paused, looked at Laura's face. She was pleading with her. There was no craftiness in her expression. Never had been. And Maddy remembered how Laura had tried to talk to her a few times, even as recently as a few weeks ago when they'd been in the department store together...

What she saw in Laura's expression now was fear, and Maddy had a difficult time dismissing it.

"Okay. You have my word."

Laura looked around, as if ensuring they wouldn't be overheard. "Gavin was just being a friend and giving me some advice. You see, I ran away from the baby's father before I even knew I was pregnant. I was so afraid he'd come after me, and I didn't want him to know where I was."

"You were pregnant when you came to Gibson?" Now that was a shock. She counted back months. It had been one of the things that had bothered her most. By doing basic calculations, it had looked as though her husband had fallen into bed with his high school sweetheart the moment she came back to town.

"Just. I hadn't even taken a test. As soon as I found out, I called Gavin at his office. He met me at my place because I wanted privacy."

"And you kept meeting that way?"

"Yes. The baby's father…you see…he's in jail. I made a lot of mistakes, Maddy, but coming home to Gibson wasn't one of them. I never intended for rumors to start about Gavin and me. He was a good friend." Tears welled in her eyes. "I was so shocked when I heard of the accident. And I wanted to set the record straight, but I was afraid. I don't want this guy to ever find me or risk anyone saying something they shouldn't, and so I let people believe what they wanted to believe. But I'm sorry about what that did to you. I can never make that up to you."

"You tried to tell me sooner," Maddy admitted. "Right after the funeral…"

"Yes. Horrible timing."

"And a few times since."

"Yes."

"God." Maddy let out a huge breath, the implications of what this meant swimming around in her head. "This changes everything. It's so… I don't know… Wow."

"I can't imagine what it's been like for you, thinking that he had an affair. And so many times I wished I could set the record straight. But it's just safer for me this way." She looked down at her daughter, her face wreathed in worry. "Safer for her."

And as a mom, Maddy understood that a child's welfare always came first.

"What was Gavin helping you with? Legally?"

"I don't want Spence to find me. Or know about Rowan."

Rowan. The baby's name was Rowan. Maddy looked down again and instantly thought, *not Gavin's. Not his daughter.* It shouldn't have made a difference. But it did. There was relief, and a lot more that Maddy would really have to sit and think about later.

"And Gavin was doing that?"

Laura nodded. "Family law wasn't his thing, he said, but he referred me to someone in the office he trusted. And he made sure I had what I needed, particularly when I felt so rough the first few months here and I was trying to find someone to hire me. No one wants to hire someone who's only available for six months."

Laura sighed and looked at Maddy. "You know we dated in high school. I trusted him…but I didn't trust anyone else. And I still don't. But I'm trusting you because you need to know. Your husband didn't cheat on you. What you two had was real. He didn't tell you he was helping me because I asked him not to, and Gavin Wallace was a man of his word."

Maddy's eyes stung. "I'm sorry," she said quietly. "I had no idea. You've borne your share of gossip, too, and it can't have been easy."

"I thought about leaving and starting over somewhere new. But Gibson is all I have right now. I still have a few friends who are behind me." She blushed a little. "And my grandparents are here.

"Anyway," Laura continued, "I don't expect us to be friends or anything. I just wanted to clear the air. To let you know you weren't wrong to believe in him." She gave a small sniff. "Gavin was so good to me, and all I've done is tarnish his reputation. That's my biggest regret, you know. I've been just sick about it. The only reason I haven't spoken up has been because of Rowan."

"Maybe someday you'll be able to," Maddy said. "If things are safer for you."

"I hope so," Laura said, meeting her gaze. "I truly do."

"I'm glad," Maddy replied, swallowing against a lump in her throat. "I'm sorry I made it so difficult for you. If I'd known…"

"Who can blame you? I'm lucky you didn't come banging on my door, ready to tear a strip off me."

Maddy couldn't help it, she laughed. And thought in different circumstances she probably would have liked Laura quite a bit.

"Do you have everything you need? For you and the baby?" she found herself asking.

Laura's face registered surprise. "Well, yes. Most of the necessities, anyway." She smiled. "Funny how I wasn't planning on being a mom, but now I'm so excited. And scared. It's a huge responsibility, isn't it?"

Maddy nodded. "Thank you, Laura. For telling me."

There was a general sense of the conversation winding up; they weren't going to magically become good friends all of a sudden. "You're welcome. Merry Christmas, Maddy. To you and your boys."

"To you both, too," Maddy replied.

Laura walked off, and Maddy watched as she went to her car and carefully extricated the baby from the carrier and tucked her into the car seat in the back.

Not Gavin's baby. Not Laura's lover. After months of trying to get used to the idea of her husband being a stranger, to find out that he was innocent put her entirely off balance. She frowned, then checked her watch. Three o'clock on Christmas Eve and she still needed to get those last-minute items. And she had a lot to think about. Because in the space of a ten-minute conversation, everything she thought she knew had been turned upside down. For the second time this year.

To COLE, IT DIDN'T feel much like Christmas Eve. Not even with his mom and dad home and the traditions in full swing. He couldn't stop thinking about Maddy and what she must be doing and how he'd blown it and shouldn't have said the things he did…

Except he'd just told the truth. It might have been rotten timing and the wrong words, but he hadn't lied. He'd fallen for Maddy, and it was too soon for her. What hurt was the knowledge that it might always be too soon. He could try to prove himself over and over, but until she was willing to trust herself and her own judgment, she'd never trust *him* to keep his word.

For the second time in the last month, he had the thought that he'd gleefully punch Gavin Wallace in the mouth—if he were still alive to take a beating.

"Is this some weird experiment where you try to light the tree on fire with the sheer power of your brain?" Ellen asked, sitting beside him on the sofa.

"What?"

She sighed. "You've been sitting here scowling for

the better part of an hour. I asked Tanner what was going on with you and he shut up tighter than a clam."

Cole smiled for all of a millisecond at that. They might have their differences from time to time, but he and his brother always had each other's backs.

"What is it? You've been quiet ever since we got back yesterday. The house and ranch are fine, so something's going on with you." She peered closely at his face. "If I didn't know better I'd say it was a woman, but we were only gone three weeks."

He looked at her, feeling miserable, then back at the tree as he let out a sigh.

"A girl? Really?" His mom perked up at that. "Who?"

He might as well talk. His mom would keep at him with as much tenacity as a dog with a bone until he told her everything. "You warned me, and you were right. I took a liking to Maddy Wallace, but it's not going anywhere. The whole thing with her husband has shaken her too much to take a chance on me."

"Oh, honey." She put her hand on his knee. "On you? Or on love in general?"

"What does it matter? The end result's the same, isn't it?"

"What happened?"

He gave her the abridged version, with enough detail for him to realize how deeply he'd gotten himself into it and how, despite the short amount of time, he and Maddy had really shared a lot. "Those boys, too," he said glumly. "God, they're cute. And a lot of work. But then when you hear their belly laughs, it's like the whole world smiles along."

He looked over at his mom, who was studying him with tears in her eyes. "Oh, man, don't start with tears. I don't think I can handle it." Not because he couldn't handle a woman crying, but because it made him feel like crying himself. Which was ridiculous, but the stinging behind his nose was a good indication.

"I warned you, you stupid idiot," she half laughed, half lamented. "I should have known better. Maddy's a good person, and you've always been one to help someone who could use a hand."

"It's not that I don't understand where she's coming from. I do. But I can't compete with Gavin. I can't make up for his wrongs. I pushed too soon and I hurt her with what I said."

"Then say you're sorry."

"It's not that easy."

"I know. It never is."

He was quiet for a minute. Then he rubbed his hand over his face and stared at the tree some more. "She told me I took her pride. It wasn't what I intended, but I didn't really consider how she'd feel. I hired her to work here and told myself I was doing her a favor because she wouldn't have accepted the money outright. I did the secret Santa thing for the same reasons. But no matter how I did it, Maddy's one point of pride in everything was that she was making it on her own two feet. And by jumping in and taking over, even in those small ways, I took that away from her. And yeah, I did it to help a friend, but it also made me feel like I was something special, you know? So how does that make my motives that pure?"

Ellen chuckled a little bit. "Oh, honey, altruism is seldom completely pure. It's satisfying to know that you've helped someone who needs a hand. It's a positive thing in a world dominated by selfishness and *I, I, I*. Don't be too hard on yourself."

"I miss her. Two days and I miss her. And the boys. I was going to ask her to bring the boys over for Christmas Eve and now it just feels like there's no point to Christmas. None at all."

"Give it time, Cole. For all anyone knew, Maddy and Gavin were happy with two precious babies as recently as seven or eight months ago. She's dealt with a lot since then."

"I know." He looked at his mom and felt a rush of love. She was so steady. So strong. He realized that all this time the reason why no other girls had held his interest was because they'd been mere shadows compared to his mom's grace and strength. Maddy was the first to come close. "It's just that I finally fell in love and I don't want to wait."

She leaned over and gave him a hug. "You," she said quietly, "are one in a million. Just you remember that."

"Thanks. And thanks for the talk. It didn't really fix anything, but at least the tree is probably safe from spontaneously combusting. For the time being."

She smiled and patted his knee again. "Your dad and I are going to the church service at seven. Are you coming?"

He shook his head. "Naw. I'll do a last check on the stock. Tanner's on call—again. But he'll be home around nine. I think we should all meet back here, have a Christmas toast, and just be thankful for our family. How does that sound?"

"Perfect," she replied. "Now, I'm going to go wake up your father. He says he needs a vacation to recover from vacation. And if I don't get him up now, he won't sleep tonight."

Cole laughed and watched his mother disappear. But when she was gone the heaviness settled in his heart again. He wanted what his parents had. He'd thought he'd found someone to have it with. But as his parents always said, it took two. And he was sitting here alone.

Chapter Fourteen

Christmas Eve church service was tradition in Maddy's family, and her parents had stayed for dinner and were going to church with her and the boys before heading home again. They'd be over in the morning around eight to see the boys, and Maddy was dreading the few hours when she'd be home alone, staring at the tree, looking at the few presents beneath it. Two from her parents, one from Gavin's folks that they'd sent up from Florida and two envelopes from her brothers, both of which she was pretty sure contained gift cards.

It wasn't that she was ungrateful. She just suspected that the magical part of her Christmas was over, done with the end of her secret Santa surprises. The anticipation was gone, and in its place she simply felt lonely.

The service was lovely as usual, with lots of carols and candlelight and smiles. Maddy sat and listened to the Christmas message and let her thoughts drift to Gavin, and Laura, and Cole, and all the stuff that had created such havoc in her life the past half year. She was so torn. She felt guilty for believing that her husband had been cheating and had fathered another child, but on the other hand, she understood that with the absence of denial came doubt. She thought about Cole and the wonderful things he'd done for her in the past month and then remembered that she'd wanted to stand on her own two feet. Was he right? Did she just have too much pride and was it getting in the way of her happiness? Or was it insecurity? She looked over at her boys, one on each of her parents' laps, and felt as if she'd let them down, too.

Laura had said that Gavin had been devoted to their marriage. Tears welled up in Maddy's eyes. She'd loved him, too. And perhaps that was why she'd been so stuck since his death. Everyone had been so convinced of his guilt that she hadn't felt free to love him, or grieve for him, or really let him go. She'd been outraged, and she'd let that take over to get her through. Because it was expected.

But she could examine those feelings, because now he was the husband she remembered. Kind, caring, willing to help a friend, even if it meant keeping a secret. Somehow, it had felt as though there'd been a final piece that just didn't fit into the puzzle, but now it slid into the empty space easily, completing the picture. And it was a good picture. Maddy understood now what Laura had meant this afternoon. She, too, had promised to keep Laura's secret, and she would. It meant that Gavin's reputation couldn't be restored. And that seemed cruel and unfair.

But she knew the truth, and that was all that mattered right now.

"Are you okay?" her mom whispered.

"I really am," she murmured back. "And I'll explain everything tomorrow." She smiled at her mom, feeling more at peace than she had for a very long time.

When the service was over, she put on her coat and reached for the boys' outerwear. Before she could get them dressed, however, Ellen Hudson approached, her silvery hair perfectly styled, the golden tan of her face evidence of her vacation in the sun. "Maddy, I wanted to come over and thank you for the help you gave out at the house while we were away."

Maddy felt awkward and miserable as she looked at Cole's mom. "You're welcome. Your home is lovely, Mrs. Hudson."

Ellen put her hand on Maddy's arm. "You've always called me Ellen. No need to stop now. Do you have a few minutes to talk?"

She looked around for her parents. "I came with my mom and dad," she said weakly. She wasn't sure if she actually wanted to talk to Ellen or if she just wanted to escape.

"We can give you and the boys a lift home. Please, Maddy. It's important."

She swallowed, anxious. If only one of the kids would fuss or something. But they were good as gold, sitting on the pew, playing with a few little toys.

"I guess it would be okay. Let me tell my parents."

"I can sit with the boys for a moment if you like. They're adorable."

They really were, Maddy admitted to herself. She'd bought them little trouser, shirt and vest outfits for church and they were scrumptious in them.

"I'll just be a moment."

And of course her mom and dad had no objection, so she had no real excuse not to talk to Ellen. Chalk it up to the second awkward conversation of the day...

She returned and sat in the pew on the other side of the boys. "Did you have a good vacation?" she asked politely.

"It was wonderful. We were so overdue for a trip away, and neither of us had been south before. We're thinking we might try to get away every year or so now."

Maddy nodded. But there was no sense avoiding the topic. "I'm guessing you want to talk to me about Cole."

Ellen met her gaze. "We had a long talk this afternoon." She shook her head a bit and gave a soft chuckle. "I warned him away from you, you know. Not because I don't like you, because I do. But every time I saw you I could see the hurt in your eyes and I knew losing Gavin had left some deep, deep scars. Particularly after certain things came to light."

Maddy wished she could defend him now. It hurt that she couldn't.

"But Cole has a thing for wounded birds." She folded her hands in her lap. "One time when he was little I found him with a crow in his lap, thinking he could help nurse it back to health. It was deader than Moses and I was pretty disgusted and washed him from top to toe, but that's the kind of kid he was. If there was a stray kitten, he wanted it for a barn cat."

Maddy's heart gave a pang. "One of the things I like about Cole is his kindness. And his gentleness."

"I'm glad you see that side of him. So you must know that he's hurting right now."

"It's only been a few weeks," Maddy began, but Ellen shook her head.

"Cole's funny that way. When he sets his mind on something, it's a done deal. And when he sets his heart on something…or someone…well, there's no halfway for him. He didn't say it exactly, but I'm sure he's fallen in love with you."

"I know."

The two words settled in the air between them.

"Maddy, I know finding out what you did about Gavin had to turn your world upside down. But loving someone means taking that risk that they'll let you down. And I get you not wanting to take that chance again, but is it worth being alone? That is, if you care for Cole. Maybe his feelings aren't returned in the same way."

Maddy picked up a stuffed toy Liam had dropped and gave it back to him. "Ellen…"

She wanted to say more but she couldn't. It was all too much right now. There were still people in the church, including Cole's father, who was sitting patiently, reading some pamphlet or something in the very back pew. The lights were soft and the Christmas tree glowed and her boys were playing and she should have been happy. But she thought about Cole and all the moments they'd shared in the past weeks and her heart just hurt. She pictured his eyes when he teased her, heard the sound of his laugh. The way he looked when he wanted to kiss her.

She thought about all the things she'd said to him and

what she'd accused him of and the pain intensified. She tried taking a breath and found herself letting out a sob. He had been kind, funny, sexy, loving, generous and understanding. So many good things. And Ellen was right. She didn't want to be alone. She wanted more afternoons in the snow with the boys between them. Oh, he was so good with the boys. Another sob broke forth as she remembered Liam putting his arms up for Cole. Liam, her shy boy, who accepted him so easily. Who trusted and felt safe.

The way she did when she was in his arms.

And the way he kissed her as if she was the last woman on earth and making her toes curl.

And how he'd suggested that she might want more children someday. She did. She still wanted what she'd always wanted—a big family, a home of brothers and sisters and laughter and arguments...

And she had turned it all away not because he'd done anything wrong but for the simple reason that she was scared...and she'd blamed it all on a reason that didn't even exist. Because he'd been too kind and too helpful.

Ellen held out a tissue. "I'm sorry. I didn't mean to upset you."

Liam came over and crawled into her lap, offering quiet comfort the way she often offered it to him. Oh, her boys. And she knew without a shadow of a doubt that if she dropped her damned pride and fear for two seconds and asked Cole to comfort her, he'd be there as soon as humanly possible with a kiss and a strong shoulder for her to cry on.

Because Cole Hudson was the kind of man a woman could rely on.

"I'm sorry." She sniffed and wiped at her eyes. "I don't know why that just happened."

"Could it be because you miss my son almost as much as he seems to miss you?"

She met Ellen's eyes. She recognized them. They were Cole's—full of compassion and understanding. And steel, when required.

"You almost sound like you want me to say yes."

"That's because I do. You're a good woman and a fine mother, Madison. You were always a nice girl. You seem down-to-earth and friendly and warm. My hesitation was because of exactly what happened. That you might not be ready for love. Yet, anyway." She smiled, a sentimental little flicker across her lips. "Cole is like his father, you know. I knew when he fell, it'd be hard. That's why we've been together for thirty-five years. And will be for many more, God willing."

"I said some harsh things," Maddy admitted. "I'm so scared, Ellen. And there are things you don't know…"

"Of course there are. As there should be."

Maddy took heart from that. "I don't want to hurt him," she continued on, holding Liam close. Luke had climbed down from the pew and was rummaging around in the diaper bag, his little white shirt untucked from his black pants. "Things happened so fast. It just scared me so much. I never imagined this happening."

"Love can be like that. Maddy, I'm just asking for you to talk to him. Come home with me and talk to him and hear him out. If he cares about you like I think he does, and you care about him the way I think you do, you need to talk. And maybe try again."

Ellen looked at the boys and her gaze softened even further. "And the twins…my word, they're sweet. I wouldn't mind having them around now and again. Will you do it, Maddy? It's Christmas Eve. There's no need for you both to be miserable."

Could she do it? Go to Cole's and ask for forgiveness for all she'd said?

Was she ready for that?

In the end she knew only one thing. If she didn't try, she'd regret it. Because the idea of not trying to make things right with Cole felt so wrong.

She'd promised to stop living in the past. Start living in the present. And she'd failed. Maybe this was the first step she needed to take to finally, finally move on. Didn't everyone deserve a second chance?

"I'll come with you," she agreed. "I can't promise to make things right. But I promise to talk to him."

"That's all I ask. I think seeing you is the only Christmas present he wants, to be honest."

They collected Cole's dad, packed up the diaper bag and put coats and hats on the boys. Maddy's mom had left their car seats in the vestibule, and the five of them left just as the last members of the women's group shut off the lights for the night.

Maddy sat in the back, in between the car seats, and politely asked about the vacation so that any potential awkward silence was filled with tales of the Caribbean. Nerves jumbled around in her stomach, wondering what she'd say to Cole, wondering what he'd say to her, wondering if she'd see him and all her words would just scatter at the sight of him. And Lord help her, there was anticipation, too. She wanted to see him again.

When she walked in the door—carrying Luke, with Liam in Ellen's arms—it seemed as though the world stopped moving. Everything went silent. Tanner was in the kitchen getting something out of the fridge and he stopped, the fridge door open and the soda can forgotten in his hand. Cole was coming through the door from the mudroom, but he halted and simply looked at her, first with numb surprise and then with the slightest flicker of hope in his eyes.

Ellen was the first to speak. "Look who I found at church tonight?"

The three of them made their way inside. "Tanner, I wanted to take a quick look down at the barn and make sure everything's secure for the night," their dad said.

"I'll come with you."

There was no real pretense; everyone was on the same page with giving Cole and Maddy privacy to talk. Ellen undid Liam's jacket and took off his mitts and Maddy figured she should do the same for Luke. And as she did Liam ran, stumbled his way over to Cole and lifted his arms joyously. "Bup! Bup!"

"Hey, little man," he said softly, picking him up, and Maddy's hands fell still on Luke's jacket. "Aren't you handsome tonight?"

Luke squirmed and she took off his jacket as Ellen disappeared to…somewhere. It was just the two of them—well, four of them. As soon as Luke was free, he, too, made his way to Cole, who sat down on the sofa and lifted them onto his knees.

"They missed you," she said softly.

"The first time I met them they just stared at me," he marveled. He bounced his knees up and down and the boys laughed. Cole smiled and Maddy silently thanked Ellen for urging her to come tonight.

"Cole…"

"My mom put you up to this, didn't she?" He didn't wait for an answer. "She pried a lot out of me this afternoon. Maddy, I'm sorry. You said time and time again that you weren't ready and I didn't listen. I pushed and drove you away. It's my fault."

She smiled. She couldn't help it. This really wasn't his fault, not at all. What he'd expected wasn't all that unreasonable. She went to the sofa and sat beside him, taking one of the boys onto her own lap. "You're a good person, Cole. Strong and kind."

"It's not that I'm afraid of working at a relationship. I know how to work hard. It's like Tanner told me a while ago—when you find the one who's worth it, then it takes work. It's not going to be easy because it's not supposed to be. And I got caught up in wanting everything right now."

"You and the rest of society," she commented. "But I wasn't fair, either." She debated on what she was allowed to tell him. She didn't want to betray Laura's confidence, especially if this wasn't going to work out. But it was so tied up in her reasons that she couldn't avoid it completely.

"Cole, I learned something recently that flipped everything I knew upside down. I'm not at liberty to explain a whole lot, but I learned that Gavin isn't the father of Laura's baby, and they weren't having an affair. I believe the source."

His mouth fell open. "Holy…wow. That's big news. How do you feel?"

"Mixed up," she admitted. "I realized that I was angry all these months, and I didn't want to believe he'd done it, but there was this weird pressure on me to accept it. I was already poor Maddy. I would have been poor Maddy who still believes in her cheating husband." It hurt to say it. She ran her hand over Luke's soft hair. "I feel relieved that the faith I had in him wasn't misplaced. And guilty because I let doubt get the better of me." She laughed softly. "I feel a lot of things. But most of all, right now, I realize that I hid behind all of that to avoid admitting how I was feeling about you. Especially with Gavin being gone such a short time."

"And me rushing you didn't help."

"Maybe, but you were so right about a lot of things."

Maddy looked down. Both kids were getting drowsy. It was past their bedtime and they were getting good snuggles and it seemed they were ready to take advantage of it.

"You were right about some things, too, Maddy. Like how I shouldn't have taken it upon myself to do all those things like I was some stupid white knight or something."

"Those things have been the best part of my Christmas," Maddy protested. "All the sweet surprises…no one has ever done anything like that for me before." It was absolutely true. "And I was completely ungrateful."

"They've been the best part of my Christmas, too," he whispered. "Because I got to see your face light up or hear your voice and I knew that for a few minutes, I'd made you happy."

Tears filled her eyes. "Oh, Cole."

She leaned over and kissed him, just a light grazing of lips, but it was the beginning of healing and starting over.

She sat back, wishing she could curl up in his arms, but she couldn't because they had the boys.

"Know what I discovered?" Now that they'd started, she felt the need to say everything. "I learned that saying you want to leave the past in the past is a lot easier than actually doing it. But it's the actions that really count, not the words. I know now that you tried to show me you cared, Cole, instead of just telling me or paying me compliments. I wasn't fair to you, but you stuck with it, anyway. And I'm so glad. Knowing the truth does change things, because you were right. It was me I didn't trust.

"But I was right all along. My faith wasn't misplaced. And I know, deep down, that Gavin would want me to be happy, to find love again and find someone who cares about the boys. And here you are. If you're willing to give me another chance."

She bit down on her lip. She'd been doing all the talking; she figured she had the most apologizing to do. But now the ball was in Cole's court.

He reached over and put his hand on top of hers.

"That is the easiest thing in the world to do," he replied, squeezing her fingers. "And I promise I won't rush you. I just want us to be together. We can take our time. I just want to be with you, whatever that looks like."

Her heart soared. Never could she have imagined this happening, not even a few months ago. But it was Christmas Eve and maybe a time for miracles. A time for truly looking ahead instead of behind. All Maddy knew was that she felt more hopeful than she had in a long, long time, and it was all because Cole Hudson had turned up at the library one day and offered to help take out the trash.

The twins were nearly asleep, and Maddy knew she should get them home, but she couldn't bear the thought of the evening being over just when they were getting somewhere. She looked into Cole's eyes and found him waiting…patiently. And she found she suddenly didn't want to be all that patient. She wanted to start on the next chapter of her life.

"Maybe you could drive us home?" she asked, swallowing against a lump in her throat. "And maybe you could stay awhile? Talk some more?" Truthfully, she thought she might like to do more than talk. Like kiss him some more without worrying about the kids between them or someone walking in.

The very idea sent whorls of anticipation coursing through her.

"Of course I can."

"Your family won't mind? It's Christmas Eve."

"They'll probably send up a cheer. I haven't been

very good company the last few days." He smiled, and it had a sweet edge to it that she loved.

She put the boys' jackets back on while he went to tell Ellen he was leaving. In no time they'd fastened the boys into the truck and made the trip into town and her house. She'd left the outside lights on, and when Cole cut the engine, Liam woke. Luke stayed asleep until she took him out of his seat, but then his eyes opened, too. Maddy unlocked the door and led the way inside, keeping the rooms dark.

"They really do need to get to bed," she murmured. "I'll get their jammies on."

Cole followed her down the hall with Liam on his arm. "I'll help."

And he did. Maddy felt a strange new contentment as they got the boys ready together. She did the diaper change while Cole fastened up their onesies and dressed them in soft sleepers. When she got bottles ready for one last drink, he cradled one child in his arms and gave the bottle while she fed the other, the two of them on opposite sides of the sofa. Maddy looked over, saw his eyes shining at her in the dark, and melted. All she'd ever truly wanted was a partner and a friend. How blessed to have found one—twice. Because Cole was that guy. Even though their relationship was in the fledgling stage, she knew, deep down, that this was it.

Together they walked up the stairs and put the boys in their cribs, covering them with their blankets. When Maddy turned around, Cole held out his hand, and she took it, lacing her fingers with his.

Once in the hallway, she quietly shut the door, and

then there was a moment where she had to decide. She could lead him back down the stairs to the living room, or ten feet down the hall to her bedroom. Indecision kept her feet rooted to the spot, but now that they were alone, Cole gently pulled her closer and cupped his hand along the curve of her jaw.

"I love you, Maddy. You don't have to say it back— you don't have to do anything. I just want you to know. I love you. I'm rapidly falling in love with your kids." He smiled, then touched his lips to hers. "But right now, I'm more focused on you. You inspire me. You make me want to be a better man. I can't promise it'll be easy, but I promise I'll do the best I can to make you happy."

She could use words at this moment, give assurances. But she remembered that words were just that and sometimes it was actions that were required. And right now she wanted to show him how she felt. Needed him to know that she was willing to meet him halfway, that he wasn't alone in this.

She wanted him to know that their relationship was a shared responsibility, not one where he gave and she did all the taking.

So she reached for the buttons on his shirt and started to undo them, one by one, pulling the tails of his shirt out of his jeans. Desire and excitement curled through her, urging her fingers on as she pushed the open shirt wide across his chest and pressed a kiss to his warm skin. He shuddered beneath her touch and she closed her eyes for a minute, being wholly in the moment.

"Maddy," he whispered, and she took his hand and led him down the hall to her room.

Quietly, reverently, they undressed in the dark, and Maddy pulled down the covers of the bed. Cole stood on the opposite side of the bed, a hungry look in his eyes. She held out her hand and they met in the middle on the soft sheets: mouth to mouth, skin to skin, heart to heart.

And when Maddy fell back against the pillows, it truly felt like a new and awesome beginning.

Chapter Fifteen

She sneaked out of bed while Cole was still sleeping. Months of being a mom meant she could hear the boys stirring; she silently slipped on a robe and tiptoed out of the bedroom, quietly padding down the hall and opening their door.

There was nothing like waking in the morning and being greeted by their smiles. Well, maybe one thing was nicer, she amended in her head. It was pretty darn fantastic waking up next to Cole.

As quietly as she could, she got the boys up and changed their diapers before taking them downstairs to get ready for Christmas morning. She turned on the tree lights and got them each a sippy cup of juice to hold them over until breakfast when her parents got here…

Her parents. Oh, Lord, she'd forgotten. And Cole was upstairs in bed…and she'd forgotten to stuff the stockings for the boys. Thank goodness they were too young to realize! She darted off to the closet for the little bags of stuffers she'd bought and hurriedly tucked them inside the little stockings.

She made a pot of coffee and figured she should get

Cole up soon so he could at least be dressed before her parents arrived. But there was no need. His footsteps sounded on the stairs and he arrived, fully dressed in his jeans and shirt from last night. There was a shadow of stubble on his jaw and to Maddy he looked perfect.

"Merry Christmas," she said softly as he got to the final step.

"It is, isn't it?" He grinned at her. "And look what's under the tree."

She turned around and saw that the twins had crawled underneath the lowest branches and had each grabbed a stocking, pulling the contents out left and right.

"And this is why nothing got put under the tree until just before we left last night!" Maddy laughed and jumped into the fray, trying to make some order out of the chaos. The boys thought it was a game and items went in and out of the stockings for several minutes until everyone was laughing.

"My parents are coming over. I understand if you want to get home." Maddy handed him a cup of coffee with one sugar. "But if you want to stay…"

"If?"

"Well, I am making Christmas breakfast. And dinner is at Mom and Dad's tonight, and I know you'd be welcome. I can't believe they were in on the secret Santa thing all along."

"They want you to be happy, too."

She curled up against his side. "Well, lucky for them," she observed. So far the boys were ignoring the presents and playing with the contents of their stockings, so she let well enough alone. "I just feel badly that I don't have anything for you." She'd thought about it, right up until the day they'd parted ways. Now she wished she'd bought some little trinket he could unwrap.

"Are you kidding? Having you and the twins under the tree today is just what I wanted. But that does remind me…"

He extricated himself from her embrace and went to where his coat was hanging on the hook. "I seem to have a little something in here for you."

Cole took a small rectangular box from the pocket. It was white and tied with silver ribbon, and Maddy accepted it with trembling hands. "Cole, you shouldn't have. Oh, gosh. When did you…"

"I bought it a week or so ago and grabbed it before we left last night. Open it."

She did, and it was a heart-shaped silver pendant on a fine chain. Nothing overly extravagant, but sweet and thoughtful and a bit sentimental. Just like him, apparently, and she was incredibly touched.

"It's beautiful," she said, laying the pendant against her palm. "Thank you so much."

He took it from her hands and unhooked the clasp, putting it around her neck. "There," he said, dropping a kiss on the back of her neck. "Perfect."

She turned around and pressed a kiss to his lips. "This Christmas keeps getting better and better," she teased, and they forgot about the stocking stuffer carnage as they kissed long and deep.

And when the kiss ended, he hugged her, which was almost as good.

"There's one thing I meant to ask you last night,"

he said when they finally went to the sofa to sit down. "How did you find out what you did about Gavin?"

Maddy tucked one leg beneath her and thought about what she could say and what she couldn't. The fear in Laura's eyes had been real. That much she was sure of.

"I can't tell you. And it's not that I want to have secrets. I don't, Cole. But I promised I wouldn't say a word, and I have to keep that promise until I'm told otherwise. No one is even supposed to know, and you can't say anything. I do hope I can tell you someday, though." She paused, took his hand in hers. "All I can say is that it doesn't matter now. I mean, I wish I could exonerate him. But I understand why I can't. And I know that doesn't help you at all." She gave a short laugh. "I guess what I'm saying is, the important thing is that it's all good. And it really is." She lifted his hand and placed a kiss on his knuckles.

"If it's good enough for you, it's good enough for me. Whatever happened, I'm glad."

"Mummm mummm mummm."

Maddy looked down to find Luke holding a square box, bouncing on his chubby knees. "Hold on, sweetie," she said, taking the box from him. At the same time she saw her parents' car pull in behind Cole's truck. "Mom and Dad are here."

"Well, then let's wish them merry Christmas." He got up and pulled her close for one last kiss. "To tide me over until we're alone again," he said, nipping at her lip.

She stood on tiptoe and gave him a tight hug. "Cole?"

"Hmm?"

"I thought of something I can give you for Christmas."

He waggled his eyebrows. "I thought you did that last night."

Her parents were coming up the walk. "Not that." She put her hand on the side of his face. "I love you, Cole."

His smile was wide and joyous. "And that," he replied, "is the best gift ever."

* * * * *

Look for Donna Alward's next American Romance novel, THE COWBOY'S CONVENIENT BRIDE, available in January 2016 wherever Harlequin books are sold!

COMING NEXT MONTH FROM

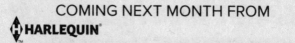

HARLEQUIN®

American Romance®

Available December 1, 2015

#1573 TEXAS REBELS: QUINCY

Texas Rebels • by Linda Warren

Jenny Walker was his brother's high school sweetheart...and therefore off-limits to Quincy Rebel. But the time has come to admit his feelings to her. Will Quincy risk family loyalty for the woman he loves?

#1574 HER MISTLETOE COWBOY

Forever, Texas • by Marie Ferrarella

When journalist Kimberly Lee is injured while working on a story on The Healing Ranch, Garrett White Eagle takes her in. But the rancher and the writer soon find that wounds old and new might just heal in time for Christmas...

#1575 THE LAWMAN'S CHRISTMAS PROPOSAL

The Hitching Post Hotel • by Barbara White Daille

Big-city cop Mitch Weston and single mom Andi Price reluctantly agree to a pretend engagement for the holidays. But when the time comes to "break up," Andi discovers she wants the fake relationship to be real.

#1576 A CHRISTMAS WEDDING FOR THE COWBOY

by Mary Leo

When bronc rider Carson Grant gets dumped by his fiancée only weeks before his Christmas nuptials, wedding planner Zoe Smart is happy to step in—as the bride! But is their relationship jinxed from the start?

YOU CAN FIND MORE INFORMATION ON UPCOMING HARLEQUIN® TITLES, FREE EXCERPTS AND MORE AT WWW.HARLEQUIN.COM.

HARCNM1115

REQUEST YOUR FREE BOOKS!
2 FREE NOVELS PLUS 2 FREE GIFTS!

⊕ HARLEQUIN®

American Romance®

LOVE, HOME & HAPPINESS

YES! Please send me 2 FREE Harlequin® American Romance® novels and my 2 FREE gifts (gifts are worth about $10). After receiving them, if I don't wish to receive any more books, I can return the shipping statement marked "cancel." If I don't cancel, I will receive 4 brand-new novels every month and be billed just $4.74 per book in the U.S. or $5.49 per book in Canada. That's a savings of at least 12% off the cover price! It's quite a bargain! Shipping and handling is just 50¢ per book in the U.S. and 75¢ per book in Canada.* I understand that accepting the 2 free books and gifts places me under no obligation to buy anything. I can always return a shipment and cancel at any time. Even if I never buy another book, the two free books and gifts are mine to keep forever.

154/354 HDN GHZZ

Name	(PLEASE PRINT)

Address		Apt. #

City	State/Prov.	Zip/Postal Code

Signature (if under 18, a parent or guardian must sign)

Mail to the **Reader Service:**
IN U.S.A.: P.O. Box 1867, Buffalo, NY 14240-1867
IN CANADA: P.O. Box 609, Fort Erie, Ontario L2A 5X3

Want to try two free books from another line?
Call 1-800-873-8635 or visit www.ReaderService.com.

* Terms and prices subject to change without notice. Prices do not include applicable taxes. Sales tax applicable in N.Y. Canadian residents will be charged applicable taxes. Offer not valid in Quebec. This offer is limited to one order per household. Not valid for current subscribers to Harlequin American Romance books. All orders subject to credit approval. Credit or debit balances in a customer's account(s) may be offset by any other outstanding balance owed by or to the customer. Please allow 4 to 6 weeks for delivery. Offer available while quantities last.

Your Privacy—The Reader Service is committed to protecting your privacy. Our Privacy Policy is available online at www.ReaderService.com or upon request from the Reader Service.

We make a portion of our mailing list available to reputable third parties that offer products we believe may interest you. If you prefer that we not exchange your name with third parties, or if you wish to clarify or modify your communication preferences, please visit us at www.ReaderService.com/consumerchoice or write to us at Reader Service Preference Service, P.O. Box 9062, Buffalo, NY 14240-9062. Include your complete name and address.

SPECIAL EXCERPT FROM
H HARLEQUIN®

American Romance®

*When journalist Kim Lee is injured on the job in
Forever, Texas, she is unwillingly taken in by cowboy
Garrett White Eagle. The journalist never believed
in love, but Santa might just write her and the rugged
rancher a happy ending this Christmas!*

*Read on for a sneak preview of
HER MISTLETOE COWBOY, the latest volume
in the FOREVER, TEXAS miniseries.*

"Well, Garrett-the-other-White-Eagle, you have no cell
reception out here," Kim complained. As if to prove her
point, she held up the phone that still wasn't registering
a signal.

Garrett nodded. "It's been known to happen on
occasion," he acknowledged.

She was right. This was a hellhole. "How long an
occasion?" she wanted to know.

The shrug was quick and generally indifferent, as
if there were far more important matters to tend to. "It
varies." He nodded at her compact. "What's wrong with
your car?"

She glanced over her shoulder, as if to check that it was
still where it was supposed to be. "Nothing, I just didn't
want to drive it if I didn't know where I was going." A
small pout accompanied the next accusation. "I lost the
GPS signal."

Garrett took that in stride. Nothing, he supposed,
unusual about that either, even though neither he nor

anyone he knew even had a GPS in their car. They relied far more on their own instincts and general familiarity with the area.

He did move just a little closer now. He saw that she was watching him, as if uncertain whether or not to trust him yet. He could see her side of it. After all, it was just the two of them out here and she only had his word for who he was.

"You can follow me, then," he told her, then added a smile that was intended to dazzle her—several of Miss Joan's waitresses had told him his smile was one of his best features. "Consider me your guiding light."

You're cute, no doubt about that, but I'll hold off on the guiding light part, if you don't mind, Kim thought. She stifled a sigh as she got in behind the wheel of her car. She *knew* she should have dug in and fought getting stuck with this assignment.

Don't miss
HER MISTLETOE COWBOY
by USA TODAY *bestselling author Marie Ferrarella,*
available December 2015 wherever
Harlequin® American Romance®
books and ebooks are sold.

www.Harlequin.com

Copyright © 2015 by Marie Rydzynski-Ferrarella

**Join for FREE today at
www.HarlequinMyRewards.com**

Earn **FREE BOOKS** of your choice.

Experience **EXCLUSIVE OFFERS** and contests.

Enjoy **BOOK RECOMMENDATIONS**
selected just for you.

PLUS! Sign up now
and get **500** points
right away!

Earn
FREE
REWARDS
HarlequinMyRewards.com
Join
Today!

MYR16R